I0607334

Terms of
Engagement
by
Susan Payne

Copyright Notice
This is a work of fiction. Names, characters, places, and incidents are either the product of the author's imagination or are used fictitiously, and any resemblance to actual persons living or dead, business establishments, events, or locales, is entirely coincidental.

Terms of Engagement

COPYRIGHT © 2025 by Susan K Payne

All rights reserved. No part of this book may be used or reproduced in any manner whatsoever including the purpose of training artificial intelligence technologies in accordance with Article 4(3) of the Digital Single Market Directive 2019/790, The Wild Rose Press expressly reserves this work from the text and data mining exception. Only brief quotations embodied in critical articles or reviews may be allowed.
Contact Information: info@thewildrosepress.com

Cover Art by *Teddi Black*

The Wild Rose Press, Inc.
PO Box 708
Adams Basin, NY 14410-0708
Visit us at www.thewildrosepress.com

Publishing History
First Edition, 2025
Trade Paperback ISBN 978-1-5092-6094-2
Digital ISBN 978-1-5092-6095-9

Published in the United States of America

Dedication

To my husband for always being by my side.

CHAPTER ONE

London, 1814

"You shot me!" Morris blurted out through a pain-induced haze.

A blurry figure sat opposite him. Pain ripped through his chest as he fought his way out of the fog from his reclining position. His shoulder burned like hell, and his throat ached with every swallow. The indistinct form wavered beside the illumination of the lamp, attired in a familiar royal blue. His assassin. A slow scan of the room gave him no clue. Provided with sparse and simple furniture, the room wasn't recognizable. Then the face became clear.

"You shot me?" He couldn't prevent the incredulity in his voice.

A pretty young woman with neat blonde curls and doe shaped eyes stared nervously at him.

"I didn't mean to." The woman lifted her chin. Defiant dark eyes filled her face, but the ripple of her long throat as she swallowed drew his gaze down. Not so old she couldn't be taken over his knee although he saw no threat in her now.

"You didn't mean to get hold of a carriage pistol, load it, cock it, and then fire at me? That sounds like a lot of accidental actions for one woman to perform. I find that difficult to believe."

"I have never shot anyone before. I was frightened, and you came in without knocking."

He grimaced as he tried to sit up further on the bed, he found himself occupying. He grumbled as he flexed muscles testing his body for other injuries, but found none. "Doesn't make it hurt any less."

There was silence, and finally she inhaled deeply. "It hurts? I am sorry. I didn't mean for it to be you."

The confession caught his attention. "Who did you think to shoot? Who were you waiting to attack in this darkened room?"

"N-no one. Not really. I was being followed, and I thought he meant me harm. I-I did not know it was you."

"Then you were right to protect yourself because I have not been following you. I just recently became aware of this address as housing a man I am interested in speaking with."

He painstakingly swung his feet off the bed and was thankful he was still wearing his trousers. Not that he was shy, but it sounded as if his companion wasn't very worldly, and he did try to uphold the propriety of society.

He noted the clean white bandage patched over his shoulder. "Who saw to my wound? This looks professionally cared for. Are you a nurse?"

"Umm, no, but I know a medical student who agreed to help me care for you. It's not as if I wanted you dead. I told you I thought you were the man following me to do me mischief. The student is very competent and close to receiving his degree."

"It would not have mattered if he was a horrible doctor, only that he be male and you could manipulate him to do your bidding. Humph, you probably made him promise not to inform the authorities either. What sort of baggage are you?"

"You needn't be rude. I explained about accidentally shooting you, and I did procure you aid, and very good aid it seems since you are able to sit and argue with me."

"That reminds me. What time is it, and where should you be? This isn't your room, so I ask again, where would you be if you hadn't shot me?" He was in no mood now that his target was out of reach. He would need to begin once again.

"Home with my aunt, but she retires very early and is used to me being out late."

"Strange. What does she think you are out doing at all hours of the night? You certainly don't look like a 'lady of the evening'."

Now that his usual excellent eyesight had returned, he could see her. She was as young as she sounded, round face with large dark eyes and golden blonde hair. A dark blue spencer with black trim molded her pleasing figure. He knew she recognized his examination of her person when she pressed her lips together in aggravation.

"That is not the point. I found you adequate, more than adequate, care and stayed with you to make sure you recovered sufficiently to leave here. The medical student said you should make a full recovery and have no lasting damage."

"There has been a crime committed." He waited to see what reaction that statement would get.

Again, the lift of her chin and the firming of the lips in a defensive move. "I don't see it that way."

"Well, you're not the one who has been shot," he said dryly. "Now where are my boots?"

She stood with both arms stretched out toward him

with the palms showing. "You should be resting for at least a day. And drink the tea I made to replace the blood you lost."

"But unlike you, I have someone who will miss me if I do not return home tonight." Standing, he didn't want to show how dizzy the action made him. He had work to do since this young woman had interfered with his evening's activities.

This time she walked nearer him and pushed him back onto the bed. Something she wouldn't have been able to do if he were not wounded and feeling the effects of having a bullet removed from his shoulder. At least, it felt as though it was more his shoulder than his chest. A narrow escape if he thought about it, and that thought made him more than dizzy.

Finding what he sought thrown over the closest chair, he said, "Hand me my shirt. I think I can get dressed and see myself home in a hack."

She stepped between him and his clothes. "You need to rest as ordered by the doctor. I can take a note round to your house to let them know not to worry about you. Then I will return to make you a meal or something. There isn't much here, but I can manage."

"You make yourself at home in someone else's lodging? Are you two having an affair?" He doubted it since she appeared untouched, but women have a way of looking innocent while being more than able to twist a knife or shoot a man when he was least expecting it.

"A, ah, affair? No, nothing like that." She turned away so she wasn't facing him any longer. A sure sign she was lying. So, she was a light-skirt after all, just not one with many years on her.

"But you are free with Mr. Haskepers' home and

food—and his bed. You are not worried to be found in this room even with a half-clothed man."

"You are, ah, more than half-clothed. You are covered except for your—umm." She waved to encompass his bare chest and stocking covered feet. "Most of you is more than appropriately covered."

"I most certainly do not feel covered." Just to be audacious, he added, "I've made love with more clothes on than this."

A rush of blush covered her neck and face as a reward. Turning away quickly, she picked up her hat, pinning it in place while glancing into the mirror on the wall next to the door.

"You reminded me, sir, that I need to be elsewhere. I will return to make sure you have not passed away from your wound or starvation." She slid through the doorway, closing it behind her.

Damn! He never got her name. That proved to him, at least, that he wasn't competent to continue with his investigation. He would need to dress and make his way home. His housekeeper could help with the wound if it bled again. His valet Taylor was good at a lot of things, but the sight of blood had him sweating bullets and trying not to faint.

He stood again, and this time his head didn't feel as if it were part of a windmill spinning in circles. He made his way to the chair and sat heavily, feeling the moisture form under his arms and around his neck from the effort it took. Hell, she may be right in that he wasn't going to make it home tonight. That would trigger Taylor to come after him and possibly scare away his prey completely. Now that he was able to think, it might have been that the young woman had left to warn her lover away from their love nest. Time lost he couldn't afford.

That was too bad, that was. He would have enjoyed a few weeks with the young lady if she weren't already involved with the man he was seeking. Morris was too fastidious to share a woman, even one as lovely as she was. The soft sound of her voice, even while irritated, didn't raise his hackles as so many other female voices did. No whining or pithiness trying to wheedle something out of a man. In fact, she showed an alarming lack of worry over what he was doing in her lover's home.

She either didn't know what the man was capable of or didn't care. Funny, he didn't get the impression she was unfeeling. After all, she had gone to a great deal of trouble seeing that his wound was cared for. Although if he had gotten an infection and died, she would be hanged on murder charges, so that may have been an incentive. If he had more time or more of his mental facilities under control, he would think on her. However, right now he had other, more demanding things to worry about.

Gingerly he pulled his shirt over his head tucking it into his breeches as best he could. Then slipped his good arm into the striped waistcoat and finally the coat he had thought to wear to the Anderson's event that evening. Well, all three sported a hole and dried blood now. Not much to salvage. They were all destined for the ragman with Taylor's tears dampening them.

He buttoned both the waistcoat and the coat one handed to keep it from sliding off his shoulder. This was more difficult than he thought although good enough for what he must do.

He forced his attention to the dresser under the mirror and pulled open the top drawer to find it empty.

He continued down the drawers to find the others just as empty. Each movement brought reminders he'd been shot. Pulling each one out, he checked the bottoms, but they were untouched, little piles of sawdust sat along the edges.

The shaving stand was the same, not even a slip of soap to give him an idea of what the man might smell like.

Walking into the only other room of the apartment, he searched for any place one might hide documents or maps. He tipped chairs to check their bottoms for recently mended slits in the fabric or signs of anything being disturbed. He checked the sideboard and found a few dishes and flatware, but nothing to give him a clue as to the man who lived there.

He could see the young lady's influence in the style of dishware—lavender flowers and possibly a hint of her fragrance, which was a mixture of violets and vanilla in the room. He hadn't been sure if he wanted to sniff her or lick her when she got close to him.

He found his hat, just inside the door where he had stood when he saw the flash of gunpowder and felt the bullet tear though his shoulder. It now sat neatly on the side-table when he was sure it had fallen with him. The young lady was organized to be sure. The entire apartment was neat although he couldn't imagine she wasted time tidying up when she met her lover here.

That meant there was a cleaning lady who came in to take care of things. If he could catch her, she may know when the owner of the apartment was usually present. He and Taylor would need to take turns watching the building until the girl, the man, or the cleaner showed up.

****

Miranda still shook as she checked on her soundly sleeping aunt, the scent of lavender and mint strong from the herbal rub the older woman used each night. The soft sounds were locked behind the door as she shut it to the click of the latch sliding into place.

She continued to her own sleeping area, the gently used furniture a welcome and homely sight. During part of this evening, she wasn't sure she would ever see this room again. How in the world had she allowed herself to become so overwrought that she actually shot a man? Even though he was breaking in, a thief didn't deserve death simply because he was hungry or needed to pay the rent to keep his children under a roof.

The district where the apartment was easily housed hundreds of such men and families. Her own purse strings didn't hold much after paying the monthly rent and buying food. Doctor bills and medications took the rest and then some. More than once, she had gone begging to her employer or to the moneylenders to cover the cost of her aunt's elixir.

Not that that was the case with the man she shot. He had been well dressed, boots of the finest grade leather with even his hose free of darns. He had been recently shaved, and his auburn hair cut neatly. Everything about him bespoke a gentleman, and that was before he regained consciousness.

Moreover, he was handsome. She found him attractive even laying there watching his blood pumping out with each heartbeat. She had wiped the hair off his brow to check his temperature and to assure her he still breathed before running to fetch Harry.

She knew the young medical student would still be

awake and studying. He was always studying—the bones of the body, the arteries and major veins, the internal organs. Miranda had found him on the front steps more than once trying to memorize the Latin terms he would be required to know before he could receive that most sought-after parchment. She had begun helping him by forcing him to tell her each bone and vein, which he often pointed out on his own tall, lanky body. They had become firm friends.

She was glad Harry hadn't questioned how a man became shot in her rooms, or how she was the one getting him medical attention. In fact, he seemed pleased to show-off his surgical skills explaining each incision and probe as if teaching a class on how to remove a bullet without killing or maiming the patient.

She had paid attention to the wounded man's torso, his muscular chest and arms that pronounced him a man of manual labor; although other than a few calluses, his hands didn't appear to be those that carried heavy crates or used a shovel. He intrigued her, and she almost looked forward to his waking up. Once he began talking or rather asking questions, she regretted her remorse for shooting him and for staying to ensure he was all right. He almost made her glad he hurt when he insinuated, she was there for some kind of liaison.

In a way, she was, but not with a man although it would make what she spent her time doing easier. Knowing what lovemaking included besides two people joining genitalia was intriguing, and she often came up against that ignorance. Often putting a stop to her whole pursuit. Getting that information from Harry would have taken her out of their usual comfortable friendship. They could talk about body parts, but not how they fit together—man to woman. She was sure Harry, even with all his classes and study, was still as virginal as she was.

Well, that was a moot-point right now. She needed to worry about what the man was going to do now he had found the apartment. There was nothing there to lead him to her, but if he waited around for his quarry too long, he would. She would need to stay away, and that would slow down her progress, which would put Guthrie out of sorts. He had given her an ultimatum, and if she didn't complete what he required, she would be in dire straits.

Not that she meant to be slow or not meet his previous deadline, but her aunt had been so ill, Miranda hadn't wanted to leave her alone in the evening. She thought she could do more, possibly take this night to catch up. Instead, she allowed her fears to control her and ended up shooting a man. At least he would live, and she had been assured by Harry without permanent damage.

Once her friend and medical student had explained all the potential problems that could occur after a bullet wound, she felt she couldn't leave until the injured man woke. As Harry ticked off blood poisoning, gangrene, loss of the use of the arm and numerous other possibilities, Miranda was so distraught she almost threw the flintlock out the window. She never wanted to endanger another person with it again.

Then she realized putting it into who knows whose hands would be worse. She usually kept it loaded and hidden in her velvet muff when she walked dangerous streets at night. She often met with men who wouldn't be seen with her during the day, but no one noted a woman and man meeting in a dark smoke-filled public room. Or paid them any attention when they put their heads together so no one could hear what they were saying. She found the method worked no matter the age of the man, or woman for that matter, although meeting with a woman was easier.

She worried about the flintlock now. She needed to clean it and replace it in the drawer where her uncle hid it for safe keeping years ago, before he died. Her aunt didn't check on it often, but the way Miranda's luck was going, tomorrow, rather, today would be a day her aunt got maudlin and wanted to remember her husband and his service to the king.

Getting out the implements, she cleaned the barrel of residue, checking the folding trigger and wiping away all signs it had been fired. Then she returned it to the desk wrapped in the soft cloth that cradled it most of the time.

She stood next to her sleeping area as the light of dawn creeped around the curtain edges. If she did a quick wash, she would still get a couple of hours sleep before she needed to wake and care for her aunt. The poor old woman didn't hear very well anymore, so dealing with the venders and paying bills was left to Miranda. Not that she begrudged the time spent on caring for her aunt, actually her great aunt. After all, the woman had raised Miranda's mother and then herself when death from disease had taken other members of the family.

Miranda snuggled under the counterpane and sighed, trying to relieve her mind of everything that had happened. All the stress and bad things that seem to come rushing up on her no matter how she tried to stay ahead of them. She felt her eyes flutter close—then shoot open.

Damn! She never got the man's name!

CHAPTER TWO

Morris snapped the morning paper open with his right hand. This getting used to having only one arm was becoming tiresome, and his shoulder still hurt like the devil. Taylor had been more concerned about the loss of the garments just as Morris thought, although his housekeeper pronounced the care of the wound itself quite good. She thought a few scars on a man made him interesting to the ladies.

After years of having her in his employ, he knew he could tease her so asked, "Do I point them out to a prospective lady friend before or during the bedding?"

The older woman waddled past, slapping a kitchen towel at him. "Now Mr. Mathews, you keep your talk gentlemanly. I know you was raised proper-like, and I'm not gonna take the blame for you backsliding into a talk sailors wouldn't use on shore leave."

"Mrs. Jessup, I'm the second son of a second son. I am so far from a title I don't even receive invitations to the season's events. I have no need to keep up appearances."

"Now that ain't true, sir. There's a pile of them pretty-smelling notes and engraved envelopes on the hall table every mornin'. I seen them myself."

Taking up the paper again, he continued perusing the open pages. "Those sweet-smelling notes are invitations of a type where the lady in question would not be averse to anything I said as long as I was in her bed when I said them."

His housekeeper left tittering saying she had never found a man so in love with his own self. He scoffed but didn't look up from his reading.

His mind wasn't on the captions or the articles anyway. They all became a jumble of words whenever he tried reading anything. His mind kept returning to a golden-haired lady he was trying to locate again. He must remember his main target, but he had convinced himself if he found her, then he would find her lover, A. Haskepers, Esq.

Then his thinking went to wanting to smash the man's face into the ground to prove he was the better man to be her lover. Knock the other man out of the picture completely. How stupid that would be. How stupid his supervisor would think it, which was worse. His cousin Westin would want him to pay attention to the main objective and worry about bedding some woman at a more conventional time.

Which for Westin before he married was anytime. Now a husband, the man had gotten scruples or something, and everyone was supposed to place the job ahead of all else. Just because Westin's wife, Emily, was an exquisite beauty with a rare sense of humor didn't mean the rest of the male world had such a wife with which to return home to.

Still, Morris' mind wandered back to that room. How she sat there looking serene and lovely with not a hair out of place even after shooting him. And someone had cleaned up from the surgery. He couldn't picture a medical student removing the bloody sheets and water. How had she done all that without being noticed?

She wouldn't have. He sat straighter allowing the paper to flutter to the floor. She would have been seen running for the doctor, emptying bloody water, or carrying out the laundry. She must have help, or she had been one busy girl all night. And although she appeared tired, she wasn't harassed or agitated. That said something about her stamina as well as her ability to think under pressure.

Calling out that he was leaving to whoever wanted to know, he grabbed his hat from the front hall. He paid little attention to the pile of envelopes Mrs. Jessup had pointed out and left his townhouse.

Paying the hackney his fare, he walked swiftly to the place he knew Taylor would be keeping out of sight of the apartment house across the cobble-stoned street.

"Any sign of her or a man who doesn't fit in with the neighborhood?"

"No, just a string-bean of a young man comin' and goin' afore dawn and sometimes after dark. Nothing suspicious about him though. He lives there on the second floor and don't talk much to anyone. Certainly, ain't lover-boy material to me, but then I ain't lookin'."

"No, I'm sure we are looking for a man closer to forty than twenty. The beauty I saw wouldn't be won over by a green youth, and besides the man we need has information only years of making contacts would glean. He must be familiar with men in Parliament to learn what he knows."

"I ain't seen no blonde doxy either. You takin' over so my dogs can get a rest? I'm in need of a necessary too unless you brought me a jug. I don't want to get pinched using the wall in the middle of the day. Even in this neighborhood, there are rules."

"No, go get yourself taken care of. I'll watch for a while since I know what the young woman looks like. Doxy is not how I described her to you." He took up a stance he learned long ago, one he could hold for hours without a leg going numb or feet aching.

"A woman who goes to a man's place on clandestine meetings is a doxy no matter how you dress her up. I know what I know, and she ain't been there visiting no one." Taylor sauntered off as if he didn't have any place to go so his departure wouldn't be noted.

Morris admired the other man's ability to blend in with his surroundings. Morris thought he probably always appeared as he was. An untitled man from a noble family—neither fish nor fowl nor fine red herring.

He tried not to stare at the three-storied brick building with the short set of steps to the front stoop. Lace-covered windows fronted the street and showed the genteel poverty most of the rest of the buildings on the block were trying to hang onto and failing. It was still safe for children to play on the sidewalk and street, but come nightfall good mothers rounded their children up and kept them inside until the morning sun assured them it was safe once again.

A rather pungent odor of refuse wafted with the breeze coming from the alley behind him, but there would be fewer places to hide if he moved. This way he could disappear down the side of the cobbler's store and be hidden from anyone on the street unless they were directly in front of the narrow walkway. He was watching people come and go, but just as Taylor said, no lovely young blonde or gentleman dressed too expensive for this area.

Morris walked back to the corner to catch a hack and

headed to his cousin's home hoping to be too early to be asked to stay for dinner and too late to have to endure tea with a myriad of his other relatives. Particularly female ones who wished to know when he would be settling down. Which meant when would he be getting married as if anyone unmarried was unstable in some manner. It irritated his sense of fairness. After all he didn't ask them how happy they were with their marriages so he could point out the fallacy that marriage would settle anyone. It was more like one must settle with marriage.

Meeting Westin in the man's office, he accepted the glass of whiskey they both preferred.

"So, how goes the hunt? I can see you became the prey at some point. Do you think our man shot you?" His cousin waved him to a chair next to the fire.

"No. I know who shot me, and it wasn't our erstwhile prey. I was so close though I felt for sure I had him or at least his lair. Now we've been watching it day and night and haven't seen him or anyone we can link to him."

"Damn shame. The men in the cabinet have held back from completing their plan not knowing whom to trust. I can't blame them since I have no way of saying it is safe to proceed."

"I know I have let you down, and others' lives depend on me finding the leak, but I must have shown my hand somehow, and the traitor went to ground."

"Getting yourself shot and bleeding all over will do that. How did that come about again?" Seeing a grin slip across Westin's face, he replied to his cousin with a hand gesture.

****

Miranda hurried home. Her head bent down letting

16

the wind buffet her hat rather than try to tear it from her head. It had been several days since she shot the attractive gentleman—that is what she called him in her mind since she didn't have a name to put to his face. She went over several scenarios as to why he had followed her to that apartment, and nothing fit. The fact he seemed to think she was meeting a man there for a rendezvous led her to think he had the wrong door in the first place. Just his luck she took such a fright she thought she needed to use the only protection she had available.

Her stomach clenched merely thinking about shooting the man, or anyone else for that matter. Next time, she would have to think longer, be sure she was actually in danger before firing. She must remember, though, she had closed and locked the door sensing the man right behind her. When she heard the slight scraping at the lock a moment later, and then a stranger entering, she meant to issue a warning. Instead, she was shocked when a bright flash emitted from her hand.

Dropping the pistol, she had been in a daze until the moan from the man lying on the scarred wood floor startled her into action. She hadn't even known the possibility of killing him had been there. She was holding the flintlock for protection, cocked it as a warning. She never meant to shoot him, kill anyone, and felt badly she had allowed her uncontrolled fears to over-rule her common sense.

Smacking into a broad chest, she realized she had been wool-gathering rather than watching where she was going. Now she held the brown paper-wrapped parcel tighter to her breast.

"Oh! I'm so sorry, sir." When she stepped to the side to move around him, she saw one booted foot move to the same direction. She thought he must have decided at the same moment to go around her, so she stepped in the other direction just as he did the same.

Oh, bother, she thought, won't the man stay in one place so they could be free of one another? She moved once more sidestepping the impediment. His hand rose, grasping her shoulder, which forced her head to snap up as she looked at him. No one was allowed to touch her at any time. It was a point of honor with her.

She came eye to eye with the man she had been thinking about, worrying over. Her eyes roamed over his body taking in the still injured arm now in a sling tied around his neck. His grey eyes pierced into hers as he held her in place with the light touch.

He said untoward to nothing, "I thought they were deep blue, but they are green and change with the light."

Caught off guard, her mind rushed to figure out how she could get out of his sphere. She didn't have time to understand the man's statement. "What?"

He stood in front of her gazing into her eyes, one than the other, with a sort of mesmerized expression.

"Let go of me, or I shall shoot you again."

She saw the grin as he dropped his hand to his side. "May I introduce myself? I am Morris Mathews and you are…?"

"I am on my way home. Allow me to pass." She did step around him but wasn't going to climb the steps to her apartment to show him her destination and continued in the same direction. When she got to the end of the block, she turned to see if the man had moved on only to find him taking his ease in front of the tenement house.

She stormed back down the street now helped along by the gusts of wind, her skirts blowing out in front of her and her spencer doing nothing to stop the cutting breeze.

"I do not wish to speak with you, sir. Please leave."

He swung his cane casually back and forth. "It is a public right-of-way, and I am not doing anything remotely disturbing. Why does my being here bother you so much? Are you afraid if I stand here long enough, I will discover the man who shares that apartment with you occasionally? Or that my being here will frighten him away?"

She tried to refrain from showing her surprise at his summarization but failed when he took note of her eyes again. She wasn't afraid of him discovering a man who didn't exist although he was still under the assumption she was here for an assignation. He didn't realize she lived on the top floor with her elderly great aunt, but he would discover her secret if he hung around much longer. Just when she thought it could get no worse, she saw Harry rounding the corner behind Mathews.

"Umm, would you care to come up to the apartment and wait with me?"

If he was surprised before, he appeared amazed she would offer him this prize. "Certainly, Miss, after you. You can fix that tea you promised me the other night."

He followed her into the wide door of the building and kept up with her swift steps. She needed them to be out of the stairwell by the time Harry entered and recognized Mathews as the man from whom he had removed a bullet.

She heaved a sigh of relief as the door's lock clicked into place behind her. She did not remove her hat or gloves because Mr. Mathews wasn't staying long. And neither was she.

"I didn't want the neighbors to see us thinking I was entertaining a man in here."

She could hear the laughter in his voice. "You mean another man. I understand them thinking it romantic for you to carry on a clandestine affair with a man who is for one reason or another beyond your reach, but quite another to explain a parade of them."

"Two is not a parade," she answered primly. Then realized her error in giving this man too much information and waited for his reply. When it didn't come, she glanced at him to see an inscrutable expression instead of the knowing smile she thought to find there.

"Do I get my tea before you toss me out because I am beginning to read you like a favorite book. Your eyes are too expressive, too revealing for a woman in your field."

"M-my field? What do you mean?" Oh, God, he did know more than she feared. That her highly prized secret was going to be blown open, and everyone would look at her differently. She would no longer be Miranda Donner, the sweet niece of naïve old Agatha Warner. Instead, everyone would know what she was, and it would change everything about her content little life.

Some would forgive her knowing she needed to put food on the table while others would condemn her for keeping such a secret. As if her very existence would contaminate them somehow. That genteel poverty was acceptable, but what if you couldn't even afford that level of living? How were lone females to support themselves? And her aunt needed medical care as well as medicines. Miranda would do anything, including taking this man's condemnation, to keep the old woman's life serene and as secure as possible.

The man in front of her seemed to want to be conciliatory. "I don't like to place harsh names on women who do what they must to make ends meet. I do need to meet with the man who rents this apartment and visits you here. I don't care if he's married or not, but I need to speak with him on matters of the state."

"You must be mistaken. The m-person who rents this apartment would have nothing of interest to the government, I can assure you. H-he has no association with anyone in government. I know. I know everyone he does." She felt justified in answering this man, and hopefully that would make him leave her in peace. It was as she supposed; there had been an error, and she had never been the subject of this man's scrutiny.

"I am sure you do, Miss, but I must speak with him directly. I take it since you are here, he will be shortly. I can wait with or without tea. It is just more pleasant with." He removed his hat and took up a seat on the sofa glancing into the room with the neatly made bed inquisitively.

"It will have to be without. I am leaving."

She headed for the door, and he jumped up, placing himself between her and her destination in seconds. The lock-hold he used on her wrist knocked the breath out of her. She scanned his eyes to see how angry he was. How much danger she was in for trying to thwart him.

"I cannot allow you to leave and perhaps warn him that I am in your little well, let's call it your little, "love nest." Although as a love nest, it has a long way to go. You could brighten it up a bit with more personalized art or decorative gewgaws. How you can meet in a place like this is beyond me. It lends itself to copulation, but not much more. Beauty and sensual things like silk covered

21

pillows should surround lovemaking. And fragrant flowers or scented candles, not odorous whale oil lamps." His gaze moved over the barren space. "And oil paintings gracing the walls. You've not added anything to these rooms during the months he has been renting it. Or is that the problem? Did he use to meet someone else here, and she took all of that with her when he was done with her? You haven't taken time to put your mark on the place yet? Should I be surprised if I returned, in say four months, to find the place changed?"

"You are despicable. Well, you can sing for your tea for all I care. I am not offering you any refreshment, and I am done speaking with you." As he loosened his grip, she turned and stormed to the small wing-backed chair. She could outwait him. She hoped she could outwait him. Her aunt wouldn't need her for a couple of hours yet and then only for a light meal. She had dispensed her medications for the day already.

So, they sat in silence. Miranda watched as the light outside dimmed and then became black. The man across from her moved, and she feared he was coming toward her. She made ready for an attack and was surprised when the glare of the lamp lit the room, and she blinked rapidly, her eyes offended by its light.

"What was it I did not contemplate? Do you two have a way of letting one another know when you are in the room waiting? Should I have lit this lamp sooner? Or is the lamp in the bedroom the one used as a message to come or leave?" He expelled a long breath. "This was a waste of time, wasn't it? As you knew it would be. That's why you weren't worried I would catch him. He will only come when you let him know somehow that it is safe. Damn, I need to speak with him, and you are the only link I have."

"You must be mistaken, sir. I know nothing about a man, nor do I believe you have any right to hold me here against my will." She tried not to let the tear roll down her cheek, but she was tired and now frightened that everything she needed to keep quiet would be shown to the world. Moreover, she was hungry because she did miss her tea, and her aunt had been alone all evening which she tried never to allow happen.

"Don't cry on me now. I was starting to believe you didn't use female wiles to get your own way. I don't want to have to believe I was wrong again."

"I don't usually cry. 'Tears do not heal, nor do they make one neither smart nor rich. Tears are a waste of life's time. Actions and words are all we have in the end'."

"Where have I heard that before? I know I picture the words in print, but where was it written? Do you know? It would save me wasted hours trying to remember."

She shrugged. "I think I saw it on a plaque in a museum somewhere. It seemed apropos."

"Possibly, but it won't get you off the hook. I need to sit down and talk with your man or my superiors will take stronger steps. I do not wish to see your name dragged through the mud of espionage. Turn the man's name over to me, and I will try to keep you clear of all charges. I don't think you are involved in the threat to the crown or even know about it. Give me the man's true name and whereabouts."

More tears joined the others, and she slowly shook her head until he huffed in exasperation and left her alone, locking the door behind him.

CHAPTER THREE

There was rapid knocking on her aunt's door, and Miranda rushed before the noise woke the older woman. She opened it to find Harry standing there with his hand in mid-air to knock again.

"The man you shot is standing outside watching our building. Can you find someone to watch your aunt? I can get you to friends who will take care of you for a few weeks." He rushed to the window and peeked out without moving the worn lace curtains aside.

"He isn't here to find me. I have already spoken with him, and he never mentioned the shooting. But you knew I shot him? I told you he was leaning against the door, wounded when I let him in."

Harry gave her a skeptical look. "Miranda, did you really think I believed you came to me and asked my promise not to talk about it because he was a stranger you found? If you had nothing to do with it, you would have called the authorities and sent the man to a hospital where a real surgeon could deal with him." He glanced back out to the street and shook his head. "We have to get you out of here. If he was all right with what we did, he wouldn't be watching us."

"No, I promise you he never asked about you. He isn't interested in you at all. He is after the man who rents the other apartment."

Silence filled the room as the two people stared at

one another.

Then Harry said quietly, "What are you going to do about that?"

"I'm not sure. I mean if I tell him and explain he has the wrong man because there is no such man, he might go on his way and no one would be the wiser. If he thinks I made a fool of him, he may try to retaliate and drag me in front of men he calls his superiors. They don't seem like a nice bunch of men, at all, since he said they would torture me."

Stepping closer, he put his arms around her shoulder in comfort. "What are you going to do? I can take care of your aunt if you want to hide with my friends."

Pulling away, she stood tall. "That is very generous of you, but you have classes and surgical theatre. You mustn't miss any of it to care for my aunt. Besides, she is my responsibility, and I won't leave her."

"I would do anything for you."

She gazed into his honest brown eyes and smiled. "I know you would, but I will not allow you to do so. Besides, we both know there is no other man to find. Eventually, he will get tired of watching me and go away. I can only think whoever he is looking for will be found somewhere else."

"I hope so, for both our sakes. I broke laws doing what I did, but I didn't want him to die. Without help he could have been dead by morning."

"I wouldn't have let it get to that point. After all, he broke into my apartment for who knows what reason. I felt there was someone following me and got to that room first. I had my uncle's gun, the one I carry when I travel at night and heard someone opening the lock. He did it with some oddly shaped pieces of metal. I found them later. I was just so frightened the pistol went off without me meaning to shoot him. I thought he would see it, turn around, and leave. I thought he was a regular burglar."

"I knew you wouldn't shoot an unarmed man for no reason, Miranda. I trust you to do what is right for both of us."

"I will think about it. If all else fails, I'll tell him the truth."

"I'll wait to hear more about this when you find an answer. Meanwhile, I'll stay low and come and go through the back door."

She walked him to the door. "That may be a good idea although I don't have a need to leave unless it is to get food—or if Guthrie orders me to deliver. I have a little ready for him, and I hope it is enough."

Once she dispersed Harry, she leaned against the door and worried. As if her slight weight could hold out a man like Mathews if he truly wanted inside. She had hoped he would have given up by now. Had decided she was a dead-end and leave her to her life. She was going to have to use the other apartment soon. Guthrie wasn't going to wait forever. He often grew quiet and then became demanding, especially if others weren't performing up to his standards. He always said she was the only one he felt he could depend upon. This was one time she wished she wasn't.

Checking on her still slumbering aunt, she went to her portable writing desk and took out a sheet of paper as well as two sharpened pencils. This wasn't how she wanted to do things, but it would have to work for now. All because some man got it in his head, she was involved with someone he thought might have information to use.

If she were a man, none of this would have happened, none of this sneaking around and hiding would need to occur. If a man shot an intruder, he could have gone to the authorities and have the wounded criminal thrown in jail. Instead, she needed to hide her activities, and now, that man was making her life miserable.

She tried to write out what was in her mind, but reality kept intruding. She found herself thinking about how to get rid of Mathews rather than how to get rid of Guthrie. Both were a bane of her existence, and she was wishing both to perdition.

****

Morris moved his feet so they were closer together and remained staring across the street at the dark apartment. He was used to long vigils, and the pleasant weather was accommodating. He mentally kicked himself for not having any other leads although he had chased some miner possible suspects only to be disappointed.

This man, whoever he was, didn't leave many signs for even the most sophisticated investigator to follow. Morris depended on the man's eventual need for his mistress to draw him back to this apartment. After all, she still visited the place since he saw her leave and return occasionally, but not any sign of anyone besides the usual, mostly elderly, tenants living on other floors.

Suddenly he saw a slip of light in the window to the apartment that his attention had been riveted on for so many days. This was it. Somehow, she had covered the window with heavy material to block the light, but that little glimpse of illumination showed her up. She was back waiting for something or someone.

Since he couldn't watch both the front and back doors, he went to the front door and accessed entry by using picks on the community lock. The dimly lit hall, most of the oil lamps being empty or the wicks burnt down, allowed him to hide in the shadows. He stealthily made his way up the flight of stairs to the first floor and waited, hoping to hear the deep tones of a man speaking. He didn't.

He saw the tattling signs of light slipping under the door shining across the hall's uneven floorboards. Stepping quietly, he stood in front of the door to the apartment and listened, holding his breath to detect any sound. If they were in the bedroom, he knew the chances of hearing anything would be naught. He hoped he would find them still greeting each other and not having sexual congress. Not that knowing such would slow his accosting of the man, but he hated to embarrass the woman like that.

If he were being honest, he hated to see her with another man even if they were fully clothed and standing feet apart. He had become proprietary and even fantasized what he would do with her if he became her protector. He didn't even know if she were already married.

She didn't seem married though nor did she wear a wedding band, and any man worth his salt would insist she wear his ring. To warn off all the others who would covet her.

She would be free to be with him once he uncovered the man she was protecting and put him behind bars. It was the only safe place for men wanting to harm the crown or disturb England's way of life. The British

Terms of Engagement

government may not be perfect, but it was one of the closest to perfection in the world.

Little by little, the common man would gain the power and make their own laws, but anarchy and sedition wasn't the way. Too many would die, and they could end up with their own Bonaparte to deal with. The aftermath of rebellion often allowed men to gain power who were worse than the ones overthrown. He had pledged his allegiance to the crown years ago, and no one, no woman, was going to get in the way of his defending it.

He knew there wasn't time to pick the lock, and with his cocked pistol in hand, he lifted his foot giving the lightweight doorknob a jabbing kick. The door flew open and slammed against the wall behind it leaving the room appearing empty at first. His stomach dropped knowing he would have to face the couple in the bedroom, possibly during coitus.

A slight movement to his side drew his attention. He saw her white face. Her eyes wide with fright and her mouth open slightly on a suppressed scream.

"What do you want? Haven't you done enough?" she accused, her eyes blinking to keep the tears from flowing.

The thundering of shoes and boots on the stairs ended when a throng of curious and frightened faces crowded the doorway. There were candles and lanterns shining into the room before he could think to shove the door back in place. A tall thin man was first to arrive, and he looked from Morris to the woman.

"Miranda, are you all right? I thought I heard another gunshot." He stayed outside in the hall blocking most of the room from the other tenants gathering behind him murmuring agitatedly.

"I'm fine, Harry. Is there a way you can assure the others all is right? That this man made a mistake and broke into the wrong apartment house. He should be on the next block. I will need to speak with him to make arrangements to pay for the damage he has done."

The lanky young man appeared to want to argue and then firmed his lips. He ushered the other tenants out of the room's doorway so Morris could shut it. Morris couldn't believe how honest she sounded, how serene considering the shock she had just suffered. They waited for the hall behind the door to become quiet before beginning their accusations and counter attacks.

"How dare you crash in here and disturb me. How dare you frighten my neighbors? I can recover from your boorish ways, but they are old and fragile and did not need their evening upset like this." She glared down her nose at him. "I don't suppose you have a badge or anything official you can show them to relieve their worries any, do you?"

"No, but then this isn't about me proving anything to you. What I want to know is what are you doing here with all these pages of documents?" He stepped closer to the dining table and picked up a sheet ignoring her outstretched hand to recover it before he had time to read. As he perused first one and then another he said in an accusatory manner, "You're scribing for him. Does he dictate to you so you can write it in code?"

"Code? Do you mean tachygraphy? I have always taken notes in short writing and then transcribed them over. I often have to take information quickly to rewrite later."

His heart dropped at her confession. Even now, he had hoped she was an innocent led by a nefarious insurgent. Instead, she was telling him she participated in the actual sedition. "You believe in this then? What you write?"

She seemed baffled he would ask. "I don't know if believe is the correct word. I put down what I hear. What the characters lead me to think they would say. How they would act in any one situation. It has nothing to do with my beliefs."

Either he didn't understand, or they were talking at cross-purposes. He grabbed a sheet closest to him and demanded, "Read this to me."

She scanned the sheet and then blushed to the roots of her hair. Not looking back at him she wet her lips trying to give herself time.

"Read it! I need to know what you are up to. How far along you have gotten things."

"It has nothing to do with you... I don't usually share my notes. Sometimes they make no sense. I write them phonetically to make them more real, truer."

"Just read it."

Blinking quickly, she began, "Most of them just want their piece and be off. Them kinds makes it better for me 'cause I can git back out to the streets afore all the blokes is taken. I git 'em and fuck 'em and leave 'em. I got real good at suckin' 'em off, and that cuts down the time considerable. Me pimp is happy as I turns 'em over quicker, and no one gets missed."

She dropped the paper and asked miserably, "Must I go on? You must have the gist of it by now. And although listening to the prostitutes in question relate these things to me was somewhat embarrassing, repeating their tales aloud to you is immeasurably more so."

He was still trying to figure out what a whore's stories had to do with taking down the crown. He now remembered how the man's name had come up in the first place.

"Wait, are there notes here about a house party in the countryside? About an hour outside of London? Who the men were that met there and how they spent their time? I mean beside the obvious."

"No, that was for the other book, so it's been stored away. I keep them all though to use as I think they should be used. What is it you are looking for?"

"I need to speak with the man you work for to find out who else was at that party."

"I can assure you the man you seek did not attend that house party, nor has he the information you want."

"How can you be sure? The author of that book has leads to several seditious events. Information men used to attempt to overthrow the crown. The royal family has good reason to fear for their lives, and all attempts upon them need to be thwarted. Now where is your lover?"

"There is no lover, and there is no man. Although after collecting this kind of information I cannot claim to be innocent, I certainly have not condoned or have knowledge of any sedition. I do not want the crown overthrown or our way of life altered by such drastic measures."

"But I have read the book. I know what he wrote."

"What I wrote, Mr. Mathews. I am A. Haskepers, Esquire. Rather, that is my *nom de plume*. I wrote a treatise about the economic problems harming orphans and widows of the country, and the publisher turned it down since a woman wrote it. I quote, 'no man would take it seriously even if he would pay out the money to buy it.' He told me he needed a writer who could get the public's attention and keep it. He threw a handwritten manuscript at me and told me that was what sold. It was a little graphic, but I understood then what he wanted."

"So, then you wrote this from what? Your own experiences?" He had difficulty believing this well-spoken lady was what he accused her of being. The high-color ebbed and flowed in her cheeks. She still didn't seem very experienced to him, and he was a good judge of people.

"Hardly my experiences. Even if I were someone's mistress, my life would be too tame. I knew I needed to do as much research as I had for my first book, so I wrote out a plan and followed it. I found a procurer, which wasn't that difficult as you know, and told him what I was looking for: an experienced woman to tell me what I needed to know to go on."

He shut his eyes wondering if she knew how dangerously close, she probably came to becoming that man's property. How easily it would have been for the swine to take her, use her as his personal whore until he tired of doing that, and put her out on the street to make him money. He opened his eyes to see her soft hazel eyes gazing back at him.

Anger filled him with her carelessness and gritted his teeth while snarling, "You are never, I repeat never, to do anything so idiotic again in your life. I will help you gather information if you must, but never endanger yourself in that manner again."

He must have made his point. She tried to pull away and drew her brows down in worry.

She spoke quietly, "You are right. Listening to myself, I realize how foolish it was to think I was safe. I now know such men have no scruples even when dealing with a lady. I need to find another way."

"A lady would not ask to speak with a prostitute to learn how 'to go on,' I believe, is how you put it."

Her fair skin showed how his words affected her as her face suffused with color.

The woman in his hands could not retain his quizzing stare. She averted her gaze, but he could tell she had taken his warning to heart. Perhaps that would save her in the future, but what was he to do now? How was he to find the trail of the man he thought to find here?

"I understand. Now." His mind wasn't on his words. He must stay on mission.

A mental shake cleared his thoughts and reminded himself he had duties to finish. His mind buzzed with possibilities.

"So, you did as this publisher asked? You interviewed, ah, this woman?"

"Yes, twice and I paid her extra. I paid the man, too, although I don't think he shares with his women very readily. She was the main character for the book, *Confessions of an English Courtesan*. Then in the two others I incorporated other women's histories into the stories."

"That would be '*Illicit Duties of a Farmer's Daughter* and umm…." He tried to remember the title of the other although he had found the Farmer's Daughter most delightful. Hayloft rendezvous and naked swimming in the brook was much more to his liking than back alley clandestine meetings. He knew the dangers and smells of the back alleys and found them unconducive to carnal behavior. "*Tales of a Lady's Maid* was the third. Is there another?"

She seemed surprised he was aware of the writings, but at the time he had been researching the author not reading for pleasure. Morris tried not to allow his thoughts to review the book's content and think of this woman at the same time. He would save that for later.

The young woman continued, "Not yet. After I wrote the first, I demanded more money. If I was going to sell my soul, I wasn't going to sell it cheaply. The publisher said he would gladly pay if I could write another similar to the first. He said he had needed to go into a second printing within a fortnight. He seemed ecstatic with the sales results and told me he has accepted discreet inquiries from women about how to find the author."

She seemed embarrassed about that, also. "That's when he decided to keep our secret very secret. He thought it would ruin the female sales, which turned out to be much more than he anticipated. Fanny Hill whetted the appetite of the public for these kinds of books, and he wanted the mystique to remain, even hinting the author was of the nobility and writing more of a memoir than fiction."

"Well, I've wasted weeks watching you to find out I had the right 'man' in the first place."

"I told you I did not write of sedition, nor do I support it in any way."

"No, but the woman you wrote about did. That first prostitute you hired. She must have been to that house party and may know each of the attendee's names or, at the least, know the other courtesans who were there with her."

"She mentioned the other women's names to me, and I made a copy. Let me find the list and see if we can find them again." She searched through some sheets with what appeared to be inky squiggles on them. "I spoke with several women and incorporated all their experiences into one woman's viewpoint."

"You find the list for me, and I'll interview them without endangering you or exposing you to that sort of environment." For some reason he didn't want her to traverse those streets she had had to walk getting the information in the first place.

"I do not think they will speak with you. I was quite honest with them and explained what I was doing. I also told them part of my profits would go to the home for destitute girls and unwed mothers in the Whitechapel area. I have adhered to my bargain of allowing them to remain anonymous. I never asked their real names."

"Well, I must find them none-the-less. Do you know the procurer's name or where he hangs out?"

"No, but I can recognize him. I used him most of the time, only talking with the women after making contact through him first."

Morris again thought of taking her with him and felt that same gut-wrenching fear for her safety. She didn't belong in those places. "He never questioned what you wanted with these women?"

"I think he feared I was a feminine activist at first. You know, trying to save the women from a life of depravity, but when I didn't try to talk the first one away from 'her life of sin,' he trusted me. If he knows all we did was talk, I never asked. It wasn't pertinent to my writing, and I needed to keep my sources available. I don't want all my books to sound alike."

He looked at her with new eyes. "I read them all trying to find clues to the writer and believe me; they do not replicate each other. Well, no more than what has to be. Copulation can only occur in so many ways—I am referring between one man and one woman or multiples of both. After all there are only so many orifices before you run out."

"I cannot believe you are speaking to me in such a fashion. I mean it is one thing to relay what I have on good advice as occurring and then another to listen to you say these improper things to me." She seemed to be honestly distraught.

"Are you trying to tell me you are still a maiden? Still innocent?" It amazed him that she could think him so gullible. "I have read the books written from those notes you so readily transcribe."

"I explained I am not innocent of knowing more than any lady should know. However, I have never been with a man. You are the only man I have ever been alone with, and that has been at your insistence not mine."

"What about the young chap, Harry. I take it he is the one I should thank for still breathing. He removed the bullet?"

"He only did it to please me, but we are just friends since we are the only two people living in this apartment building under the age of fifty years."

"You needn't keep lying to me. You no more live in this apartment than I do. There are no clothes and only food for light eating. Nothing of which to make a meal."

She became quiet and refused to meet his gaze. A clear sign she was going to tell him a falsehood.

"Miss Haskepers, I implore you to stop lying. If I cannot trust you, then I feel I must turn you over to the authorities. I don't wish to bring their wrath down upon your head if you are as, you tell me merely an author.

The government has found more traitors since the Six Acts were passed than any other time in our nation. I do not wish you tainted with that if you are, in fact, innocent."

"I do not know how to prove I did not do something—only that I did. I will take you to the woman who first told me of the house party you speak of and no other. You do not need to know everyone I interviewed. After all, I did promise not to get them into legal problems or trouble with their procurer although I never promised him security. He probably thinks he has something to blackmail me with."

She wrung her hands as she continued to speak, "I would not put it past the man. My aunt would die of mortification if she learned what I have been doing to keep us fed and pay for the medicine to help with her breathing problems. I have been trying to get enough saved to move her to a safer area in a country village. There is less soot there than in the London air, and all the doctors blame the poor quality of our air as adding to her distress."

"But you leave her alone?"

"I have Harry take care of her sometimes when I need to leave and she wasn't well. He can do that without interference with his studies."

"I take it he is close to receiving his degree?"

"Yes, but he would take the extra time to see to her needs. He is short of funds, and I pay him for the care. I live on the top floor with her. I made the publisher include this apartment as part of the recompense for my stories. I needed a private place to spread out my notes and work on my manuscript. After I wrote the first book as he requested, I told him he must publish both or neither. I wanted to secure my place as a legitimate author, as well, under my original *nom de plume*, M. Scott." She sighed. "As he predicted, my original dissertation hasn't brought in any money to speak of."

"But it is where I read the quote. You wrote that and I remembered it for a reason. The book was informative, but certainly not as diverse as these others are. Salaciousness will always outsell political tombs."

"I know that now, and although I sometimes feel a certain taint creeping over my skin, I take secret pleasure in knowing something I created is in the hands of so many. My publisher assures me it sells mostly in the Mayfair bookstores to the gentry and not in the less desirable establishments on the fringe of society. I didn't want to think I aided in some woman's downfall. My books always have a sense of injustice which I want the reader to take away with them. Women have such few choices. One misstep and they can find themselves in a life that is repulsive."

"Each piece of fiction has its place in society and yours entertain in a unique way. Titillating and educational. I didn't realize how what you wrote about and how you wrote about it made me see the occurrences in a different manner. There is a sort of tilting at windmills and making the women appear as any other except living through a horror not usually of their own making." He viewed the woman in front of him in a different light. "I recognize your energy trying to explain not only what these women do, but why they do it. And how they found themselves with no other option due to society's rules and foibles."

"Not so much the first one. I was quite shocked with the first book, but by the time I wrote the others, especially the Farmer's Daughter, I was quite adamant she was coerced into doing what she did by forces outside her control. Societal prejudice and illogical manner of blaming the female while ignoring the male's equally bad behavior. Or worse, as in that story when the blighter took her innocence and left her with a babe in her belly after promising marriage."

"You are right, of course, but we are unable to alter that sort of thing tonight. I will return for you here tomorrow evening, and we will find the procurer and the woman you first interviewed. Who should I ask for at that time?"

Without hesitation she said, primly, "Miss Miranda Donner, plain Miranda Donner."

He let himself out without waiting for her agreement. He didn't wish to think about taking her into that sewer of Whitechapel, but he needed her to lead him to the right pimp. There were too many men, too many dark corners for them to hide in if he tried to find the correct man on his own. At least Morris would be by Miss Donner's side as protection this time. He wondered if she had taken the flintlock with her the first time?

CHAPTER FOUR

They climbed out of the clean hackney cab. No wonder the driver glared at them in disgust when Morris gave their destination. The man probably thought a clean, well-dressed couple such as he and Miss Donner appeared would be heading to a less controversial area. He scrutinized the dark lane carefully as he guided her down the pavers stepping around things he thought questionable at best. The stench of the place was almost overwhelming although his companion made no faces or complaint.

"You are sure it was this corner? They all begin to look alike without signage," he warned as she set the brisk pace.

"Yes, we are quite close to where I found the man each time I searched for him. I found keeping one's eyes alert to ensure people know you are paying close attention to things about you while keeping-up a goodly stride to show them you know where you are going keeps them at bay. Otherwise, one can be compromised in the most impolite ways. Men down here are no gentlemen; I can assure you. Even those who arrive in crested coaches."

"You were accosted, Miss Donner? You failed to mention that when I asked."

"No, you seemed to focus on the woman's procurer who I found more honorable than the men I ran into during my interviews on the dissertation. Now that is a story that needs writing—the men who spend hours debating over the ills of this district while at the same time fully enjoying its variable kaleidoscope of women and questionable activities."

He knew the problems of this part of the city and how those in charge work toward keeping it as it is rather than helping people out of their misery. It wasn't what he needed her to focus on, so asked, "Explain to me how we will find this woman?"

"I pay the procurer and tell him the type I want. He has them meet me in a room he provides. I wait there until they show up, and then I explain I only wish to talk with them and that I will pay them for their time."

"And that worked? No one tried to rob you as you left or the women didn't try to talk you into more?"

"No, do they you?" She turned her head to peer at him, and he felt the heat of a blush.

"We are not speaking of me. I am a man and can handle myself if confronted. You," he waved his hand toward her as if that explained everything, "are certainly not made to protect yourself. I hope you have your pistol with you, and that you had it with you that first time as well."

She glanced away from him. "I didn't think of it the first time since I had no idea what I was getting into. Now I never come down here without it. That is why I am wearing this cape. I will shoot a hole right through it if I must."

He realized her right hand was wrapped in the side of the cape. He thought it was to keep it from flopping. Knowing she was armed and knowing first-hand she would fire if she thought she was in danger lessened his worry. Between the two of them, they would be able to fight their way out of most attacks.

"There." She made a slight tip of her head toward a dark corner. "That man with the cap pulled low over his eyes. That's the man. Let me go over on my own, or he might get frightened and run away. He won't show himself again until he knows we are gone."

"That wasn't the plan," he said tersely.

"I know, but now that I'm here I see the way people are watching you. As if you're a police officer or something."

"Or something. But I'm not stepping away. I'll stay right here until you make contact. Then I'll join you."

She gave a brief nod and went directly to the man he knew had been paying close attention to them. As she approached, the procurer didn't turn and disappear into the surrounding crowd going about their daily business. Some heading home now that dusk was about to fall. Not many, even those living here, wanted to face the people who called these streets home after dark.

The pimp kept his head down although Morris could tell Miranda was speaking earnestly to him. Her hand never left her cape which Morris took comfort in. Finally, he felt she had been on her own long enough and joined her. He could no longer hold back without knowing what was being said. He trusted her, but not the man, and if she said something to frighten the pimp away, she was correct in thinking the parasite wouldn't be back. At least not to this corner.

As he approached, Miss Donner glanced up and said something comforting to the pimp, he was sure.

"That'll be more for the two of you. Even if one only wants to watch," the little man said with a leer.

"That's fine. Here, double the usual amount, is it?" she asked as if she were buying ribbon.

She peeked up to meet Morris' eyes half pleading, "I need you to pay the man, dear. He wants his money up-front."

He swallowed at the lump forming at her softly worded request, "Certainly, darling. Now what exactly was that?" He put his hand into his pocket to select the right coins.

After being given a room number in a nearby apartment house, they went there to wait.

With natural grace, Miranda walked toward the building, which must have been familiar to her. She explained the room numbers changed according to the customer's request. He glanced around making sure no one was paying attention to them as they entered through the grimy front door. The worn wood of the halls bore centuries of scuffs and scars, the walls once painted a bright color now faded to a sooty ocher. He placed his hand on her back as she led the way to the room.

The door lock turned easily with the key she had been given, and he stopped her from entering the dimly lit room.

"Wait here. I want to make sure there's no one hiding in here waiting for a dupe." He entered, his Liegi Derringer in his hand and searched under the bed finding the thin mattress unable to hide even a slender person. The faded tattered curtains couldn't conceal any one either. Beside the one dirty window, there was a washstand with a pitcher of water sitting next to the bowl. An oil lamp hung from a brass hook in the wall near the door with clothing hooks on the opposite side. There was no artwork or even a chair.

He waved his hand offering Miss Donner a seat on the threadbare counterpane. She smiled at him gratefully and sat daintily on the edge, paying no attention to the unknown stains dotted over the surface. He grimaced and felt a cad for allowing her to accompany him to this place. It was little more than a bordello, and she was a respectable lady even though her career choice could have been considered more thoroughly.

He began to wonder if the nefarious man had taken advantage of them. "Do you think the…" A soft knock at the door interrupted him.

Miss Donner stepped forward and opened the door before he could indicate she stay out of sight from the hall.

She peeked out and said, "Oh, it is you. I'm so glad he sent you to me, Lucy. How is your daughter? Did she like the dress I brought her?"

"Oh, yes, milady, she was right happy to get it. The other was so tight, and she is getting to be all arms and legs she is." The newcomer stopped abruptly when she saw him. "Oh, you've brought a man. I thought Mr. Phineas was mistaken when he said there'd be two of you. Said one just wanted to watch. Is that true, milady?"

"Don't worry, he is a friend who is interested in what I do. You know, how I gather my information for my books."

The young woman with bleached yellow hair and large expressive eyes stepped in with a worried expression on her face. "If'n you say so, milady. I don't want any trouble."

"I would never allow Mr. Smith to cause you any problems. In fact, he paid for this meeting and will leave a hefty vail as well when we are finished."

"What do you want me to do for the money?" the young girl asked. He judged her as not having reached twenty years of age although her looks would not last much longer in this way of life.

Morris was anxious to be done with the meeting. "You told, umm, the lady about a house party you attended in the country. Can you elaborate on the attendees?"

The young woman stared at him and licked her lips. He realized his error. "Who else was there with you? Do you remember any of their names or titles?"

Her face relaxed, and she replied readily, "Oh, yes, since it was the first time I ever met a marquis and three earls. I never been in a house so grand, either. It was beautiful with black and white marble squares in the entrance and a huge dance floor with mirrors along one wall opposite lovely glass doors that led out to the gardens."

"Can you remember anything more about the house? Were there stairs up to the front door, or did it have turrets?" He coached knowing he should allow her to tell him these things on her own. Remember at her own pace, but he wanted to get his information and leave as soon as possible. He had never felt in danger like that before, so he put it down to having a novice with him. Miranda didn't belong there, and he hated that he needed her.

"No stairs. The carriage let us all out, and we walked through two wide black doors. There was a lion with a ring in its mouth on the doors, both of them. The butler wasn't nice at all, but the other men were all right."

He interrupted her speech to ask, "Yes, about the men. What were their names again?"

He noted Miss Donner held a small notepad and

pencil ready to write the names. He knew she had already taken down the pertinent information concerning the house.

Lucy began again. "I was with several other, ah, friends from Whitechapel. Most knew one another from working together or attending various parties. Not all of us were Mr. Phineas' girls, just three of us. But he didn't come with us which he sometimes does to make sure he gets his cut."

"Who were the other girls? Can you get us a meeting with them? We would pay." He offered wanting to know anyone he could question about the house party.

"Loraine and Millie. Loraine's dead. Died of the pox soon after, and that's a worry for all of us 'cause we often shared a customer. It makes me think about getting out of this work completely." She couldn't hold back the shudder that went through her body.

"What about Millie? Is she still alive?" he asked seeing the possibilities of finding these other women slip through his fingers.

"Millie left and went back home. She said she would gladly milk cows rather than do what had to be done here to make a living. I agree, but I have my daughter who lives at a home for the destitute right now. I get to see her, but I can't take her out, not even for a few hours. They don't want me to be able to sell her to Mr. Phineas or someone like him." She appeared hurt and worried tears filled her eyes. "I'm her mother. What mother would do that to her own child?"

Miss Donner patted her hand. "You're a good mother. Emma knows you love her, and that is the most precious gift a mother gives her daughter."

Lucy nodded, sniffling and wiping her cheeks with

the back of her hand.

Morris escorted Miss Donner to her apartment with the promise she would transcribe her notes for him, although he remembered every name Lucy mentioned. Even names Lucy wasn't sure about, he had recognized the men she had described. His nerves were on fire. He was anxious to get this list down on paper as well and get in touch with his contact in the government.

He needed to make sure they understood not all the names he collected were necessarily part of the insurgency. Some may simply have been invited for cover, and he didn't think any of the muslin-set was involved although the ladies present wouldn't be ruled out. He was still trying to figure out the house. Some of it sounded familiar, but there were several homes that the rooms described could belong in. He must find the right one that contains all such rooms and decor.

The evening was just beginning, and he needed to change and get back out to the gambling hells and dubious parties to find some of the men on the list. He would need to track each one down and talk with them individually to rule them out of the equation. Men in their cups and out for an entertaining evening at a brothel were more likely to speak honestly about their politics. After all, in those sorts of places friends and like-minded men always surrounded one.

Morris could not believe his luck. He had run into several of the men already and mentally scratched them off his list, although he had passed their names on to his superior. That man would be just rising and dressing for his day on the floor of Parliament. Morris wiped his hands over his eyes. They felt gritty from the London air, and he smelled like stale tobacco and even staler ale. He hungered for his bed and a dreamless sleep.

That wasn't true. He yearned for the comfort of his bed, but also the comfort of a woman in it—one particular woman. When he finally realized there was no man keeping Miranda, his heart had beat double time. He had felt it throb inside him. When he realized she wrote those books, that she knew about enjoying sex outside the marital bed, he felt light headed and fought to keep his hands at his sides. When he realized she was free to become his lover, his mouth went dry, his groin tightened, and his manhood heated. But he wasn't as free. Not at this time, anyway. He must push all those thoughts and feelings aside and concentrate on finding the anarchists.

As he arrived home, having done all he could do without more sleep, he wished there was more time to convince the lovely Miranda they should continue to work together closely. As in his bed, working toward the same goal of pleasure. His groin tightened again. If that kind of thinking persisted, he wouldn't fall asleep for hours.

CHAPTER FIVE

Miranda finished the notes and then concentrated on all that had occurred in the few short hours prior. She had been unmasked as the author of risqué books, had returned to the bowels of the city she hoped never to see again, and spoken with a man who made her skin crawl as she knew he dealt in selling human flesh which was not his own.

However, good came out of it. Lucy got a bit of money and perhaps Mr. Mathews would help Lucy get out of the city. After all, he seemed sincere in needing the young woman's help to find the house as well as identifying the right man when he was apprehended. Mr. Mathews' promise to move Lucy and her daughter to a safe village where they could live quietly was the life-line Lucy needed.

That should have made Miranda happy, but for some reason it didn't. All she could think of was that she would no longer be needed. Mr. Mathews wouldn't drop in unannounced and make her heart flutter with anticipation. He wouldn't gaze at her with those storm-grey eyes making her want to loosen her corset and possibly other items.

Miranda knew what her body was telling her. She had taken notes on making love too many times not to recognize the signs of desire. The women she spoke with said it was rare, but occasionally, the men who paid them also made them gifts of their bodies. She became aware they would do most anything for this special man without payment. Most men did not have to do so, but the women said the desire was an extra bonus and made the time with these men enjoyable.

She toyed with the idea of taking Mr. Mathews to bed, ruffling her fingers through his hair and stroking his chest and arms, which she knew were muscular. After all, she had seen him stripped to the waist and the tightly fitting breeches hadn't kept her imagination from running rampant although she admitted to not knowing exactly what men had beneath that layer of clothing.

A smile crept across her face although she felt no shame. One thing she had learned and understood was that sex was meant to be fun, to be enjoyed, to ensure a future generation. Only the *ton*, those who thought interbreeding with other social strata would somehow weaken the future generations, put such constraints on it. On the other hand, she thought too much inbreeding caused weaknesses. The Bible warned about too close of a blood relationship between married couples for a reason.

How in the world did thinking about Mr. Mathews undressed lead to giving birth to new generations? There was no chance of wedding him or forming an alliance where children would become a part of their lives. He may want to bed her, but never wed her. Afterward, it would be the story of her life. She was the only one with control of her body, and she would keep it that way.

Not having a procurer for protection, she knew better than to give her life away to a man who only saw her as a bedmate. When he tired of her, she would be less than the lowliest of the women she interviewed. Possibly a new story plot, but not one with a happy conclusion.

****

Miranda trudged up the last flight of stairs. The calves of her legs aching with the last bit of strength. There was still work to do to feed her aunt and help the poor woman into bed. At least Agatha went to bed early, which would leave Miranda with her thoughts and worries over the next book. As she lifted the key to the lock, the deeper murmuring of a man's voice and the higher ones of her aunt could be heard. Harry must have stopped by to check on Aunt Agatha. Miranda pushed the door open with a lighter heart. Seeing Harry always eased her mind. Knowing there was someone to depend on to help her aunt was a Godsend.

She was surprised to see not only her aunt sitting on the sofa, but Mr. Mathews sitting in the chair next to her. A pot of tea and several plates were in front of them on the tea table.

"Why, Miranda dear. I am so glad you made it home before Mr. Mathews needed to leave. We have been enjoying this grand tea your friend brought. He even steeped the oolong to perfection."

Miranda turned her attention to the man who seemed to dwarf everything else in the room as he merely smiled benignly. "I travel about quite a bit and most other countries do not know how to make a decent cup of tea. I learned to do for myself or go without."

"I am sure you did not make these dainty sandwiches." Her aunt took another nibble of the crustless piece of bread in her hand. "The salmon mousse is wonderful although I must admit I prefer the *foie gras*. I haven't had pate' for so long, and it has always been a favorite."

Miranda forced herself to focus on her aunt. "I didn't realize you had a partiality for it, Aunt Agatha, or I'm sure in this district of so many *émigrés,* I could have found you some."

"You do so much for me already, dear, I don't want you to think I was in need of anything. In fact, I am not, but to taste such luxury again is a pleasure." Agatha smiled toward her benefactor benignly as a queen bestowing knighthood on a favored cavalier.

Mr. Mathews nodded in acknowledgement of the appreciation. "It was my pleasure to furnish you with this little treat. I sometimes find the need of conversation when I dine, and I have found the best in you."

Her aunt actually blushed then smiled. She appeared so much younger at that moment. Miranda could see her relative as the young beauty she must have been. Had the older lady become too isolated in these upstairs rooms? Was the old woman merely waiting to die? Had Miranda failed her aunt by keeping them both locked up in this solitary apartment building? Even if it was safe and sound?

Aunt Agatha covered a yawn behind her hand and murmured an apology. "This grand meal and the lateness of the hour have tired me. I apologize for leaving you at such short notice, but please stay and keep Miranda company. I know you really came to speak with her and were gentlemanly enough to settle for a lonely old woman."

Morris stood to help the older woman from her chair. "Nonsense, I enjoyed every moment of our talk. It is amazing as to how many acquaintances we have in common."

"Even though most of mine are doddering old folks

or buried six feet under. Now I must bid you farewell, Mr. Mathews. Please stay and finish your tea. I'll have Miranda back out to you in a thrice."

Miranda helped her aunt walk into the only other room in the apartment. She pulled the dress off over the old woman's head and a night rail on. She left the wool stockings in place but tucked the bedroom slippers beneath the edge of the bed as usual.

"Now don't fuss with me, girl. Get back out there and keep your very handsome friend company. He speaks very highly of you and your abilities. How long have you been working together? You never mentioned you have a young man in your life. Don't let this one get away." Another yawn interrupted anything more her aunt wanted to say.

"He isn't a young man in my life, Aunt Agatha. I'm not sure why he came bearing gifts, but I did help him with a special project recently, and this might be his way of thanking me."

"It was very well done of him. Don't miss eating one of those macaroons. Quite, quite, tasty…" Aunt Agatha was asleep for the night.

Now for facing him. Miranda pulled back her shoulders and lifted her chin.

"What could have possessed you to come here and with a full tea as well! I didn't want things to be more complicated than they were, and I arrive home to find you having tea with my only relative. The one person I care about even more than myself. How will I explain this once she begins to think about how odd it was that a stranger appeared out of nowhere bearing luxurious gifts?"

"It's simply a tea. I assure you I have enjoyed such

repast from my housekeeper's kitchen many times. I'm glad so many items met your aunt's favorites list. Of course, the women are of the same age, and that might have accounted for the similarities in taste. I much prefer roast beef and a hearty mustard to *pâté*."

"You are trying to divert my ire onto some poor unsuspecting housekeeper. It was not she who brought this repast and set it in front of my aunt like *manna*."

"I don't think this has to do with the tea as much as it has to do with who brought it."

She turned from him and stalked to the window, seeing the shapes of the other tenements across the street in the dusk, no streetlights would shine on these corners, no night watch calling out all's well. "I am mad at myself for not knowing she liked *pâté de foie gras*. For not realizing, I am not enough in her life. She looked so happy, so much like her old self sitting here when I came in." She turned back to find him standing close behind her. "I might have done this all wrong. I should have kept her in the neighborhood where she felt comfortable, where her old friends could visit…"

"Do you have the funds to do so? Did you then?" His question made her realize she left because she didn't have enough money to stay in the quiet area of London they had lived in and still pay for the medical attention her aunt required.

"No, but if I give up the other apartment here and if my publisher would extend early payment, I could find her better lodgings, possibly a place with meals included. There would be other people in her same circumstances there. Women widowed and left with few choices."

"And then where would you live? How would you eat?"

"I would survive; I always have."

He pulled her into his arms and covered her lips with his. She tensed and then relaxed, having wanted to know what it was like to kiss such a man, be held close by such a man, for a moment believing she belonged to such a man.

He sucked her bottom lip into his mouth and let it slide out, tracing the delicate inner skin with his tongue. She sighed, and his tongue entered her mouth as she hoped. She wanted to taste him, have him in her even if in so slight a way. She touched his tongue in return, and he moved his hands to her buttocks, pulling her into his arousal. She knew what that meant. What she must be feeling. Desire. She had heard about it, had written about it, but this was the first time she had experienced it.

And she did desire this man. Wanted to be closer, wanted his touch on places hither unknown to a man's touch. Thoughts of things she knew could occur between a man and woman flashed through her mind, and she wanted them all, to try them all with this man. Allow him freedom with her body, trust him with her very life if he would continue to touch and kiss her as he was doing.

"I knew you would taste like this, feel like this. I can hardly stop myself from tearing these clothes off you and taking you on that bed in the corner."

The reminder they were still in her shabby little apartment was like having a pail of cold water thrown over her. What was she thinking? He was still the man who used everyone for his own needs, and she was still the tired virgin too stupid to protect herself, her heart, from such a man.

He must have realized something changed and stopped kissing her but left one hand cupping beneath a breast and the other pressing her hips tightly to his arousal.

"So, you began to think. I knew it would be dangerous to allow you to do so, but I want you to listen and then decide whether to send me away."

Miranda remained staring at his somewhat wrinkled cravat.

"I want you to know I did not expect this when I brought the tea. I thought it would be a good way for the three of us to get to know one another since what happens between you and I will most certainly affect your aunt."

She nodded slowly unsure where this was going, but hoping she would not hate him or herself by the end of the conversation.

"I like her, and I think she deserves more than life has dealt her, dealt both of you. No one considers the widows. How little is left to them. Especially ones without a title or lands. Even war widows are left to fend for themselves. It's disgraceful."

"I know this and found it of no benefit. My aunt's friends seemed embarrassed when they ran into her since she could no longer dress well enough to go out in the evening. When she fell ill, I think many of them wrote her off as dead."

"Let me buy her a cottage in a nearby village, one outside the smoke and soot of London. I'll hire a woman to live with her, make her meals, and care for her as needed."

Her heart swelled with his generosity; tears filled her eyes. "Oh, Morris, you would do that?

"I may be the second son of a second son, but I have more money than a nabob to my family's dismay. I can

Susan Payne

spend it, as I like. In addition, I can afford a house for you in Mayfair, not far from my own. A few blocks which I can walk whenever we wish to be together which will be nightly for the first few months. I promise." He seemed moved to kiss her then, her mind still trying to make sense of what he was saying. "You can visit your aunt when I'm called out of the country or for a day or so when I'm tied up with work. You won't be cut off from one another completely."

"So, you'd take care of me in this Mayfair house?" she asked as her mind stumbled over what he was making her into, wanting her to do to keep him in her life and in payment for her aunt's continued welfare.

"Of course, anything you want. Servants, a carriage and team, the newest fashions. I would love to dress you as you should be dressed," he told her enthusiastically. He bent to cover her mouth again, his thumb stroking a nipple through her bodice.

"And I could continue to write?"

"Nothing too controversial. We don't want anyone to look into who A. Haskepers is, you know." He kissed her neck, sucking gently.

"I see. I can be your kept woman, your mistress, your whore, but heaven forbid I get caught writing."

He stepped back. His brows drawn together. "I said I didn't care if you wrote. What more do you expect from me?"

She peered up at him, trying not to admit her heart was breaking. "Nothing. I should have expected nothing more of you than what I received. For some reason, I placed you in a separate category than most men, most men of the peerage at least."

"I don't understand. Isn't this what you want? I

58

mean my offer may have been unplanned, but not my intentions. I want to take you and your aunt out of this place, put you where you will be happiest, where you belong."

"A second son of a second son evidently is too high for me to look, so perhaps I should look elsewhere. My aunt will have to settle for what I can offer her, and I will keep with what I can provide for myself, just as I've been doing. And you, MISTER Mathews, can leave us both alone."

"Perhaps I surprised you making all these plans without your input. Perhaps you need more time, or if I've left something out, I'm sure we can come to some arrangement...."

"Arrangement? You want an arrangement? And what happens to me when you are tired of this arrangement? When someone else catches your eye and you want to spend time with her? What if there are children?"

He seemed confused by her questions. "I have never created a bastard, yet. I'm very careful. Besides, I thought with all your connections you'd know how to take care of such things." He shook his head as if clearing his mind. "The cottage will belong to your aunt along with a stipend for her and her companion. The townhouse will be in your name. What more can you want?"

She observed the man she thought she loved. "Nothing, what else could I expect after all? A house in exchange for the use of my body seems more than fair considering women like Lucy get less than a shilling. And I won't even have to give a cut to my pimp—merely my body."

"That's unfair; it's not the same, and you know it. I care for you. I want to be with you. I didn't make this offer lightly."

"I understand the honor you think you've bestowed upon me. However, I'm turning it down, and I do not expect a repeat of this dishonor again." She strode to the door and opened it, making her intentions clear in case he was still confused.

Firming his lips, he grabbed his top hat as he passed the side table. "If you change your mind, I will give you time to rethink your answer."

She prevented herself from slamming the door. Why disturb the other tenants merely because her heart was broken and the fool she thought she loved was nothing more than a man who thought like most men—with his prick.

Turning down the lamp, she undressed in the dark as usual, lifting the dress over her head and laying it on the chair to keep it as wrinkle free as possible. She climbed between the sheets shivering. Not just from the lack of heat, but from the reaction to him, to the man who thought so little of her he would proposition her using her aunt's health and happiness as bait. Did he think so little of her capabilities he thought she would jump at his attempt to make her into one of those women she tried to help out of such positions?

It proved he didn't know her. Didn't understand anything she wrote in her books if he thought his offer was anything she would have contemplated. She was so angry her threatened tears dried in her eyes. Scenarios of what she should have said, how angry she should have gotten, what she would have done if she had the loaded flintlock on her person danced through her mind.

She was as angry with him as herself for thinking he was different. He saw a woman in need and thought his offer was all that it would take for her to trade her body, her soul for creature comforts. She shook with the rage rushing through her and thought never again. I will do for my aunt and myself, and I will never again look toward a man for help. She hated both him for putting that carrot in front of her and herself for even considering taking a bite.

CHAPTER SIX

Morris woke early and resisted riding over to see Miranda even though it had been days since they last spoke. Although he wanted to see her, speak with her, he knew she wouldn't have anything new to add. He would let her steep for another day or two before making another offer. If she had something particular in mind, why the devil didn't she just say so?

He continued searching out the men Lucy mentioned as attending the country house party. He hadn't told either woman about the death of one of the men mentioned. That death being the reason for his superiors ordering him to consider the case.

The man, Trowbridge, had arranged a meeting to confide what he knew about a conspiracy of the highest order and the plan of starting a revolution similar to the one France had endured. Only it promised to be less drawn out since the planners had learned from the French.

Too much leniency in the new government had brought about the death of thousands of the common Frenchman. It had been meant to free those people from the aristocracy and their never-ending demand for more riches made on the back of the common people. Now that Napoleon had set himself and his family up as new nobility, the French appeared in charge of their own lives. Many Englishmen found that attractive.

Before the meeting or information could be passed on, the man had been found dead under suspicious conditions. Poison by the looks of it, Morris had been told. It was up to him to find the culprits Chesterfield was going to inform upon before an attack could be made on the monarchy.

Morris and many others blamed The Six Acts put into place. They worked right into insurgents and anarchists' hands. One by one the acts removed freedoms common Englishmen had enjoyed for decades. The prevention of any gathering of more than a few people, allowing government guards to enter private residences to search for and remove all weapons, and making it illegal to use firearms or march even for practice was like a red flag to a bull—a very angry bull. The people could see their freedoms which they held tightly to their hearts were being taken away.

The monarchy reacted as if the people had risen-up against it when in fact they were merely stating their displeasure at higher prices and lower availability of basic foods. No one besides the very rich and nobility could afford to feed their families, and those rich did it on the backs of their tenants. Too many similarities to the state France was in before their problems.

He shook his head to clear his thoughts. It didn't matter why or if those involved felt justified. There could not be the same sort of revolt in England as occurred in France. The smaller nation could not weaken or other countries would take it over and no one would have any rights. The House of Commons as well as the House of Lords would be demolished while the heads of other countries sat on the once English throne.

Grabbing the now creased sheet of paper with the

names crossed off, he continued his hunt. He would find the men involved in this insurgency and end it quickly. Then he would have time to focus on the book that began this hunt and its author, the delectable Miss Donner.

Before he could finish with the list, a request to visit headquarters brought him new information. It seemed things were in motion, and many of the same men were planning to attend another country party, courtesan's et al. This time Morris had been invited and not because he was friends with the others. The invitation came because of whom he knew, whom he was known to work for among the aristocracy, and his reputation for keeping what he did private. He accepted on behalf of himself and his newly acquired paramour.

He rushed to the tenement house and up to the second-floor apartment. Rapping quickly, he was anxious that she open the door. He heard movement behind the scuffed green door and knocked again.

Miranda opened it, a wary expression greeting him. He pushed past her and closed the door to prevent any interruptions from her neighbors. As usual, there were sheets of paper piled neatly on the table surrounded by notes of squiggly lines and dots.

Unlike his usual suave self, he blurted out, "I need you."

She stared at him as if he had two heads.

"I mean, I need you to come with me. Stay with me."

Her eyebrows arched, but still she remained mute.

"Don't turn away. I'm here on a purely business basis. An arrangement I am hoping you consider seriously for the safety of the royals."

"It seems like the visit to my home was also a purely business arrangement. I got the feeling that those were the only kind you entered into."

He ignored her sarcasm. "I have received an invitation to the same country house Lucy attended, and I need a woman to come with me as my paramour. Every man must bring at least one woman. You are the only woman I trust to allow me the freedom I need to do what I must once we get there."

****

Miranda couldn't believe Morris was here and never mentioned that offensive proposal of *carte blanche*. He seemed to have forgotten about his vulgar offer all together. She woke from the trance she had sunk into.

"And just what does that entail, Mr. Mathews? I thought we straightened out your misunderstanding of what I did versus what I write about. That things between us were settled."

"I did; I do. I need a woman who will not expect me to dance attendance upon her and to sleep with her at night. I need you." He seemed to realize his plea was being ignored. "I will pay you, of course. I need a presentable female to pretend to be my paramour. I will pretend that I do not wish to share since we are new to one another. The others will understand. Women are brought and sometimes shared and sometimes accommodate only one man. They do not wish an unaccompanied man since he could cause problems. Although if a man brings more than one woman, it is acceptable that one or the other would circulate."

"How magnanimous of you all and almost egalitarian in concept. If you leave out the fact that many of these women began in the business against their will." She turned from him wishing this entire debacle wasn't being played out in the middle of her apartment. She would have difficulty not remembering it long after he was gone.

"I'm not here to argue the rights or wrongs of the system. I don't have anyone else to ask, and it begins in six days. I will use the time there to search the house for any signs of a plot or evidence. It gives me access to everyone since the men rarely bring their valets to these things. One is furnished to shave the men, and there are lady's maids for the women. It is easier for me to get about without running into people."

"I wouldn't need a maid." She was intrigued about getting closer to the men she wrote about and how she could use this offer to her benefit. This would be much more information than she could get through a second party. She could see how the men treated these women on a first-hand basis.

She continued, "We must have an agreement and rules. A term of engagement much like an employment contract between us. This is purely a business arrangement as you so rightly said before."

"Well, what say you? Will you attend this house party with me?"

"Nothing else? No ulterior reasons for me to attend with you?" He shook his head, a bland expression on his face. No sign of his ever offering for her as a mistress.

She could use the money, and she would have the book in to the publisher by then. "Harry could take care of my aunt, and I could pay the doctor ahead for his visits. I think that will work out. But I will not allow you any liberties."

A smile broke his expression. "Good. I'll pick you up tomorrow morning first thing."

"Wait, I thought you said it wasn't for six days."

"We have much to do. I have to get you dressed." He rushed as if expecting her denial. "Although you look perfectly fine, people will expect a woman on my arm to be dressed in the height of fashion."

"I can't afford to buy…."

"No, but I can, and I insist. If it makes you feel better, you can sell everything afterwards and give the money to the home for the destitute you sponsor that you think I don't know about."

"I don't need much. A dinner dress is all. I have day dresses."

"You have day dresses suitable for a clerk or shop girl—not a courtesan. You will have to sparkle and keep the other men's minds off what I may be doing. The women are brought as entertainment for all, but as I said before, I will keep you close."

He replaced his hat and left before she could formulate any other questions or protestations.

Miranda was ready and waiting in her writer's apartment when the hackney drew-up to the front. Peering out the window, she spied Mr. Mathews descending the cab and went to meet him, not wishing anyone to become too curious and ask questions when she returned.

"I wish I knew more of what was expected of me. I barely slept a wink worrying I was missing something. I don't wish there to be any problems, Mr. Mathews."

"Why not try calling me, Morris. After all, we will be thought to have a very intimate relationship, and although it will be new, we must act the part of close friends, very close friends."

"That may have been part of my insomnia, too. I mean how friendly do I have to be, or pretend to be?"

She toyed nervously with the tie on her reticule.

He appeared to take her question to heart. "I know I am asking you to pretend to be my paramour, to pretend to be fascinated by me, to pretend to find my lovemaking amazing. Pretty much what the other women are there for, except the men with them think the women are sincere whereas I will know you are not."

She nodded, worried he still wasn't explaining everything, but he had been to these types of parties where as she had not. She wrote about them through the eyes of paid women like Lucy, and that girl explained there was a lot of acting going on. Miranda straightened her back against the squabs of the cab and knew she could do what he asked of her.

The hackney pulled up in front of a respectable dress shop, and Morris helped her alight. She looked up at the two-story building. The exceptionally clean bay window displaying modestly designed dresses and hats pleasantly surprised her. She began to think she would enjoy this splurge of the budget. Her new book would soon go to press, and she could afford a new dress and possibly pelisse.

A bell sounded as Morris opened the door, and a slender woman came out through a curtain. Her stern expression turned to one of great happiness as well as affection. "Morris, darling, how I have missed seeing you." The French accent was fake, but Miranda liked the woman whose joy in seeing Morris seemed legitimate.

"*Mademoiselle*, I have not been in need of your services, but as my note informed you, I do have this lovely lady with me who is in need of a full ensemble for a weeklong house party. Treat her like a newborn babe emerging from the womb. She will require everything from the skin out, and when you think you have enough, add a tad more."

"Riding ensemble, *monsieur*?"

Morris smiled benevolently. "I said everything."

The modiste nodded as she took out her tape measure and notepad.

Miranda interrupted. She didn't want a riding costume and wasn't prepared to pay for one. "I don't ride." Morris turned to look at her with one eyebrow raised so she repeated, "I don't know how to ride a horse."

"No matter, most of the other women won't either, but they will still dress the part when the men go on the hunt. There is always at least one day set aside for hunting, and we must not let the others leave us behind. It wouldn't be polite."

He again raised one brow in question as if daring her to argue the point.

She followed the modiste behind a curtain and stepped onto the raised dais where an assistant helped her disrobe. Soon she stood in just her long chemise, full corset, and stockings.

Suddenly there was a bevy of women holding fabrics up to her skin and taking them away when they were displeased with them. She held out her arms for more measurements, a seamstress's dress form was brought in, padded and cinched to model Miranda's shape which she must admit from this angle wasn't too bad.

A hush came over the room as Morris came in holding some pages of fashion plates.

"I think we should keep things subtle, *mademoiselle*. Like this only drop the neckline just a little, but keep it respectable." He turned toward Miranda who tried to melt into the background, narrowed his eyes, and then studied the drawings once more. "I think keep to the gem tones such as ruby and emerald. Em, rhinestone trim not pearl. She's too robust for demure pearls. I don't want to be accused of seducing an innocent." He smiled to take any sting from the comment.

He stared up at her. "I knew there was more to you than that dark gray frock you wear was showing. You won't recognize yourself once Mademoiselle is through with you."

"That's what I'm afraid of. What is all this going to cost me?"

He didn't turn back around but glanced at their audience. "My dear, you are worth every sovereign. This is no more than what is expected, I assure you. And as for repaying me, I can think of several ways."

Her entire face burned with embarrassment, and knew if she gazed in the mirror across from the dais, she would resemble a ruby. Licking her lips, she thought thoughts she would never put to paper, and she wrote books that were banned in many bookstores.

A young store clerk draped her in fuchsia with some sort of silver thread woven into it. The modiste pinned and tucked until Morris was satisfied.

He smiled in pleasure. "That's perfect. She will need four, no, five evening gowns similar to this one. Not too many ruffles or lace. Although she's young, she's far from an ingénue."

"Yes, sir, I understand what you are looking for," the modiste replied.

Miranda was about ready to let her words blow them all to kingdom-come when the modiste waved her arms and all the cloth, trims, stockings, and shoes disappeared in a mass exodus of shop girls.

"We are done, madam. The dresses and accompaniments shall be to you beginning tomorrow."

Morris answered, not looking to where Miranda was thrusting her arms into her own dowdy frock and pelisse. The feather on her hat appeared withered and forlorn after hours of being surrounded by the glorious creations brought out for Morris to review.

She was surprised to see so many nearly completed dresses, including a riding habit of turquoise trimmed with silver ribbon on the collar and sleeves, and a morning dress with a bronze and cream striped skirt and matching spencer. A lacy cravat was included to wind around the thin throat of the cream blouse.

The modiste said she should expect that tomorrow. The problem was that they were being delivered to Morris' home address.

Miranda lost track of the number of dresses and gowns discussed and hoped Morris didn't expect her to be grateful for the dressing of her. She was supposed to be home by now, and she was just re-dressing. There would be no time for writing today since her aunt would wonder why she was gone again. Miranda would have to stay with her aunt until that woman fell asleep.

Her eyes threw daggers at the man she now felt had taken advantage of her need for extra cash and in a way, her patriotism. She smiled at the dressmaker as she left; after all, it wasn't the woman's fault Miranda was kicking herself for agreeing to this ridiculous scheme.

Who in their right mind would mistake her for a...a professional? A woman beautiful and coy enough to trap the great Morris Mathews? The man thought himself worthy of a paramour of the most desirable and fashionable of women. Didn't he have eyes in his head? Did he think she was going to fool anyone let alone a house full of men who were connoisseurs of such women?

Pulling her arm out of his helping hand, she mounted the cab's step and flopped onto the leather bench. He entered and watched her from the corner of his eye.

"I have offended you. I'm sorry. I apologize if you are willing to accept it. I was acting as a lover, a man dressing his mistress. I thought you understood that. We must stay in character whenever we are together now. Modistes are great gossips, especially if they think what they know will build their own clientele. Mademoiselle dresses many of the petticoat set. In fact, some of the dresses she fitted to you are coming from a mistress of a man whose wife found out about his liaison. The lady cut her husband's allowance since she was the one with the coin and he only had the title.

"Did this modiste tell the wife?"

"I'm not sure, but then again the wife is sporting a good number of the dressmaker's designs while the mistress is not." He stared out the window as they passed from the shopping district to the seedier section she called home.

"I like her better for doing that, but I do not like the feeling of having all those shop girls and seamstresses thinking that I, that you and I, ah...."

"I understand completely, but there is nothing so remarkable about today for them. I am not married nor engaged and as for you, they don't know who you are. You could be a woman fresh from the country, and I have made you an offer that is hard to resist. As gossip fodder, it's not very successful. It will not make the tabloids I assure you."

Her stomach sank thinking some friend of her aunt might read of such things and look up the old lady simply to rub her aunt's nose in her niece's fall from grace. "Is that possible? I mean that my name will be linked to yours and then exposed?"

He swung back to face her. "You make it sound as if I'm the devil, Miss Donner. Again, I don't have much of a reputation to protect, but I'm not a man who abuses or mistreats his liaisons."

"That will be little comfort if my aunt thinks I've been compromised. If she realizes it has to do with paying for her care...then it will break her heart."

"I am not indifferent to you or your aunt's feelings. I will do nothing to make what we are doing public, and I assume you will not either. Therefore, the chance of anyone hearing about it, let alone writing about it, is a moot point."

"I guess it's too late to take back my agreement? You have already ordered all those gowns and dresses..." She was torn between wanting to help him with his assignment and with saving the royal family even if they would never know versus protecting her aunt who has not set foot out of the house in months or had a visitor from their old life in years.

He sat there so smugly. "I will take your silence as agreement we will continue as planned. The clothes are being delivered to my townhouse, and you will make a stop there before we head into the country. Everything except your travelling clothes will be packed and ready for transport."

CHAPTER SEVEN

Everything had been planned to the inch. Harry was in charge of looking after her aunt. Aunt Agatha thought Miranda was travelling to an old friend's wedding in Bath. Since it was so far a distance, Miranda would be going early to renew the relationship and then return to Soho after the wedding breakfast.

Miranda was anxious, nervous, and excited. She scanned and studied all her notes of the interviews of the prostitutes, focusing on what Lucy had told her about the house party and how the women spent their time. It was a revelation, and she hoped Morris knew what he was doing. She didn't want to be put in the position of having to duplicate even a few of Lucy's experiences. She wasn't that good an actress even if she understood all that Lucy had told her.

Dismounting from the cab, Morris' footman came out and paid the hackney. She felt the center of attention entering a bachelor's establishment even in the middle of the morning. She thought of going to the side door and pretending to be a vendor of some sort, but the waiting footman put an end to that.

In the foyer, a mature maid curtsied, introducing herself as Sally. The tall room boasted white marble tile floors while polished stairs curving elegantly led to the first floor. Miranda followed the older woman to a fashionably decorated bedchamber. The wall coverings were of yellow and white daisies while the counterpane was white rucked linen trimmed with a wide satin ribbon. She remembered chambers like this from her youth but hadn't been in such a room for years. Perhaps her make-believe friend who was getting married in Bath would have a room such as this.

As the maid instructed, Miranda disrobed down to her skin and quickly dressed in the lacy chemise trimmed with a pink ribbon tie which covered her to below her buttocks. She eyed the corset. The maid returned and helped pull the strings tight, giving an extra pull after telling Miranda to exhale. She wasn't sure she could breathe, but all thought of personal comfort was forgotten as the maid brought out a gorgeous ruby red travelling gown.

Once on, the lacy bodice showed more of Miranda's breast then she was comfortable with, and she continued to pull at it.

"Now miss, this is exactly as it should fit. Nothing is showing that shouldn't be showing."

"Are you sure? I don't think anything fit like this when I was at the dressmakers." She turned to the side, but from every angle, she felt naked or at least as if she was wearing her undergarments alone.

"I am quite sure, miss. I dressed Mr. Mathews' sister until she married and moved to Scotland with her new husband. As much as I liked the lady, I can't sleep sound in a country where the men don't wear breeches."

Miranda refrained from pointing out the maid's fraudulent thinking and continued to try to tug the dress's neckline higher. Finally, she gave up, allowed the maid to restyle her hair, and couldn't fault what the woman did. Sally had piled the curls on top of her head enhanced by a faux hairpiece to give her own soft blonde hair more volume. It made her appear more mature, worldly. Miranda liked not looking like a schoolgirl any longer.

The matching ruby red velvet hat with white ostrich feather pinned in a curve gave her a flirty little peep hole. If she wished, she could practice her few talents on Morris as they travelled to the country party. He would be able to tell her beforehand if she was making a fool of herself or not.

****

Miranda glided down the stairs like a duchess. Morris' mouth went dry, and he tried to swallow, his Adam's apple feeling as if it were choking him.

"Very nice. Very nice indeed, Miranda. I am more pleased with our choices than I can say."

"Your choices you mean. You and the mademoiselle seemed to have chosen everything between you." She tugged on her gloves. She would not meet his gaze, and he wondered where the once very brash woman who possessed the audacity to shoot him had gone.

His gaze brushed across the top of her bosoms, but he was smart enough to know he made her self-conscious. He didn't wish or need her to be skittish and back out of their arrangements now, so close to his getting access to the very house that may be at the core of the plot against the crown.

Instead of the usual hackney, there was an enclosed carriage waiting for them outside the home and a footman there to aid them. Miranda sat in the front facing seat, and Morris sat beside her. He felt they needed to be on a friendlier footing if they were to fool anyone into believing they were intimate with one another, let alone man and mistress.

"I have found out a little more about the others. I thought we should take this time together to review them and make a mental list of who is the most likely to be part of the plot and who is merely decoration to hide the others' activities."

She turned toward him. "I agree. I will feel more in control if I know as many of the players as I can. I am half afraid the women may be ones I know or have interviewed if not tried to talk into leaving their profession and procurer behind."

"I doubt that the ladies accompanying these gentlemen would be of that ilk. They all seem to be professional courtesans and well taken care of while under the man's care and once she has been given her conge."

"Conge? As in getting sacked?"

"These things happen. There are usually gifts such as jewels and property if the relationship was of any duration. It is known they all end eventually."

"And the woman has no voice in these, um, endings? It probably follows the man finding a younger, newer bedmate. A newer opera singer, a younger actress."

"Don't blame the way of the world on me. If the woman didn't want to make the agreement in the first place, she needn't have to."

"No, she had so many other options it must have been a difficult decision." She snapped at him and stared out the window as the town began to roll behind them, and the streets became quieter.

He realized he might have hit a nerve, reminding her of his botched proposition. One he felt had been foolish and improbable right after the words left his mouth. He had just been so sure she wanted him as much as he wanted her. So sure, she was of the same thinking that men and women can come together for pure enjoyment and when it ended, it ended. Both free to leave whenever that time came.

"Miranda." She didn't blink. "Miranda, listen to me. We are not entering into any such agreement. This will not end with me leaving you destitute and possibly bearing my child. What others may have agreed to or done has nothing to do with us. We are on a mission, and we are incognito to do so. Do not paint me with the same brush you use on these other men. The men attending this function and the men in your books."

"But you have kept mistresses, women you paid to sleep with you." Her voice sounded strained as if she were keeping it under control.

It was his turn to stare out the window, ignore her earnest green eyes. "I have admitted to you that I have maintained mistresses, and when it ended, it ended amicably. They were widows who left after deciding to accept an honorable offer. I gave them a parting gift for all the pleasant nights we spent together, but I never sacked them. It wasn't that kind of arrangement."

Her shoulders slumped. "I apologize. I guess I am on edge, and we have digressed. You were going to tell me about the men at this house party."

"Yes." He, too, needed to focus on the mission. "The host is an earl, Lord Stanhope, who has rented this house several times before and always to hold a weeklong party like the one we are going to attend. His mistress acts as hostess while his wife is with her lover in Sussex."

"I think I need my note pad to keep all of this straight."

"No, simply worry about who is there. You won't

be expected to know the Debretts on these people. Merely to look and act besotted with me. It will keep the other men at bay, and I will ensure they know I do not wish to share since we are new to one another."

"I understand. Who else should I know?"

"Viscount Reynolds, Lord Wyngate, and Sir Thomas. They are the three who were at the last three parties and brought different women each time. There is another agent trying to find those women and ask them about their time there."

"No one else? How many are going to be present?"

"There are to be eight men. I am unsure how many women. As I said at least one each, although Lord Stanhope may have hired extras as he did with Lucy." He thought this time was as good as any. "You'll be known as Jewel, simply Jewel. None of the ladies has a title, and they will be using a first name only. This way no one will link you to this party unless you tell them who you are. I would suggest you keep that to yourself for obvious reasons."

She turned away from him watching as the trees and pastures rushed past. His driver was making good time, and they would get there in plenty of time to talk with the other guests before dinner. He hoped he would find his insurgent as quickly as possible. There were questions Miranda hadn't asked him, and he wasn't sure how she would respond once she realized he had been withholding facts.

****

The carriage turned a sharp corner, and Miranda found they were travelling on a tree-lined road covered in crushed stone ending in a well-manicured lawn. A white granite folly stood in a garden area, and the sun showed on the coat of a roe grazing in the distance. The house itself was breathtaking, easily housing fifty sleeping chambers. The cream-colored stone contrasted with the stone of the drive and the green grass kept scythed short. The double central doors were tall and boasted the lion-head knockers Lucy remembered.

She leaned out to count the stories and then the windows along the front. Four stories and forty windows. And there were only going to be the eighteen of them, more or less. How were they to search such a mansion even if they took the entire week to do so? It didn't seem as if the two of them could complete the feat. She wasn't even sure what she would be looking for. She needed a mantra. She was there to make it seem as if Morris was simply another guest wanting to enjoy wine, women, and song.

Miranda hoped she hadn't made the biggest mistake of her life. What would a man involved in the overthrow of the monarchy be prepared to do if he thought he was being watched? Or that a novice endangered his plans?

The carriage rocked to a stop, and she took a deep breath only to be reminded how tightly she was tied into the corset. She glanced quickly over to her companion to find him watching her.

"You aren't going to let me down now, are you?" His gray eyes pierced her for the truth.

She raised her chin shaking her head. "We have an agreement, and I won't let you down."

The door snapped open, and a liveried footman bowed them into the house where a stern butler announced their names as if they were entering a ballroom. A man who must be their host, Lord Stanhope, entered the foyer, the black and white checkered floor leading up the double staircase and through the wide doorway from which his lordship had emerged.

"Morris, so glad you could accept my invitation." He paused as his gaze roamed over Miranda's form from head to foot and back again. "I see you have brought a beauty with you. I was told you were a connoisseur of lovely ladies, and I see I have not been misled."

"Lord Stanhope, I would like to introduce Jewel. She is lovely and a new addition for me. Please don't be offended if I make it my duty to see that she appreciates only my attention. She did not come cheaply."

Stanhope laughed and slapped Morris on the back. "With a beauty like that I completely understand. I think I would keep her for myself for at least the first month or two although there will be many who will get their noses out-of-joint. This is supposed to be a friendly house party, and that usually means sharing one's property."

Miranda felt herself bridle although tried to control the tide of color she feared was going to show through the rice powder Sally insisted she use.

Morris turned to her. "Jewel, I know you wanted to pretty yourself up before meeting the others. I'm sure there is a footman or maid who can show you to your room. I'll come up to lead you in to supper later."

She forced a smile to her lips and nodded then curtsied to Lord Stanhope in pleasant agreement. She picked-up the skirts of her dress and followed the butler up the stairs.

****

Morris entered the sleeping chamber without knocking. "I wasn't sure you were alone, and I thought the maid would find it odd I knocked before entering."

"She was here when I arrived but left when the bags

arrived for another couple."

"Which drawer did she unpack your corsets into?"

"I sent her away when the trunks arrived. I thought it would be best to stay more private so no one will suspect anything if we acted differently than she expected. I mean, we need to search rooms you said, and we need privacy to do that. I don't really need her. After all, not all the courtesans travel with their own maids. She didn't seem to find it suspicious. Perhaps she thinks I've never had a maid and don't know how to treat one."

"Probably for the best. My personal valet knows what I do, but I don't need him to care for my daily needs. I've been known to shave myself without slitting my own throat." He pulled the curtain aside to check what was out their window. Nothing of interest so he glanced around the room instead.

"I see they placed your trunk in here with mine, but I'm sure we can find a footman to move it into your room." She continued to unpack, hanging the dresses in a large room fitted with shelves, drawers, and hooks.

He stopped reaching for his cravat and said evasively, "That might be a problem." He peered around the sitting room and found a two-person sofa, two chairs, and a table. Nothing that would accommodate him for a night's rest.

Meeting her gaze, she began to shake her head. "Oh, no, you tell the butler you need another room. Tell him you snore. Tell him I snore. I don't care what you tell him, but you and I are not sharing a bed. You promised this was simply for show."

He waved his hands to calm her. "Sh-h-h-h, we don't want anyone to hear us fighting. We're supposed to be newly besotted with one another, remember? If I were to sleep in another room, leave you in here on your own, you wouldn't be alone for long."

"I'll lock the door. There's a key in the lock right there." She pointed to the hallway door to prove her point.

He took a key out of his pocket and waved it at her. "And I have a key that opens every room on this floor."

"Oh, how did you get that?"

"From the home's owner, and it cost me a pretty penny, too. The gentleman owns this house to bring in funds, and he rents it to anyone who can pay and that includes selling the keys."

"I can't believe he's so deceitful. How does he know you won't do something nefarious with that key?"

"The man rents to Lord Stanhope knowing what kind of house party he hosts. Why would he get squeamish if one of those guests wants to gain entrance to rooms other than his own?"

She thought about it then continued, "It doesn't help our predicament. I won't sleep with you."

"Miranda, we won't be sleeping with each other. We will merely be sleeping in the same bed." He spread his arms to include the large carved four-poster bed with canopy. The blue of the curtains continued to the coverings as well as the wallpaper. "Look how big this is. I will stay on my side, and you will stay on yours. How can that be a problem? Do you think I don't have control of my baser instincts?"

"It's not that..." she said slowly, glaring at the wide mattress from one side to the other.

"You don't have control of your baser instincts?"

She smiled knowing he was teasing. "It just seems so wrong. How can I face my aunt after this? How can I face the world after this?"

"Neither will know. We will know the truth. That nothing happened to lessen your value as a woman, and we are doing this for the best of reasons."

"I suppose so. I guess that means you will see me in my chemise again." She shook her head slowly. "That really cannot be acceptable behavior no matter what the reason."

"I won't tell anyone if you won't. I'll die with the secret. I swear to you." He covered his heart with one hand, a grin playing around his lips.

"I know I'm going to regret this, but I put my corsets in that drawer. Why do you wish to know?"

"I have something to hide and a corset drawer usually goes unsearched even by the most diligent of spies."

She huffed. "I bet you never let one go unsearched."

"That is as may be, but I hope anyone interested in me will ignore your underclothes."

CHAPTER EIGHT

After all was said and done, Miranda allowed the maid to return to help her keep the hairstyle Sally had created for her. Only instead of the hat, a glittery-feathered concoction sat in her hair. The evening dress was vivid lavender with silver trim. The modiste must have accepted Morris' suggestion of not using pearls. The gossamer wrap she carried low on her arms did not hide the charms of her bare shoulders. Silver earbobs dangled almost to her shoulders drawing the eye of any observer to her long neck and porcelain skin.

Morris returned to dress and lead her into supper. They were all to meet for the first time in a parlor where the women would be on display, and the men could proudly take credit for bringing the loveliest of the lovely as their companions.

Miranda held onto his arm and felt her fingers quiver. He didn't say anything but gazed at her giving a reassuring smile. That was how he entered the parlor, with a smile on his lips watching his companion closely. If he planned it, things could not have been better. He appeared as a man completely smitten, she thought. Quiet an actor after all.

The introductions were over quickly. As Morris predicted, the woman used only first names with little explanation of who they were except for whom they were with. The last woman, Caro, barely acknowledged the introduction of Morris, and she sniffed at Miranda rather than truly acknowledged her.

Miranda thought she must be imagining things at first. Was that a nipple? Both nipples? My God, why doesn't someone say something to the woman? They all appear to be her friends. Miranda felt herself tense and peer around for other's response and found no one seemingly embarrassed or even ogling the poor woman's bosoms.

The conversation continued without comment, and Miranda finally realized everyone had seen the nipples, probably numerous times, and they had become blasé so to speak. Not a man among them took a second glance at the woman, although they made Miranda feel like a juicy piece of lamb in the butcher's case. All the men seemed to find her bosoms worth watching, perhaps hoping her nipples would suddenly jump out and wave at them.

A giggle tickled her lips. She refrained from laughing, even smiling and kept the same serene expression on her face that the other women seemed to simulate. She dared not glance over to Morris who she heard talking in a natural way. Politics became the conversation point, and the women paid no attention at all, not even pretending to attend to the men who paid them to be there.

The butler announced dinner and the men and their Cypriot harlots lined up regardless of rank and protocol was dispensed with other than the host and his mistress led the procession. There were name cards on the table, and Miranda found herself sitting at the opposite end of the table as Morris and realized she would have to play her unfamiliar part on her own. She could not depend on his injecting a proper answer for her or interceding if she became embroiled in a conversation, she should have steered clear of.

The man to her right was Lord Wyngate who she remembered was one of the men Morris was most interested in. She planned ways in which to get him to reveal his true beliefs. Morris told her to leave the 'spy work' to him, as he put it, but then why was she there if not to help? She was an investigative researcher and should be able to conceal her real reasons for talking about anything while gleaning the truth.

She smiled in what she hoped was an encouraging manner. So out of practice at flirting, she wasn't sure if she ever knew how. The clean-shaven gentleman rewarded her with a drawn-out gaze followed by a quick wink as his other seating companion drew his notice by bumping into him as she sat.

Once the women took their seats, the men took their chairs so some semblance of social propriety was observed at these dinners. The man to her left was a heavily mustached gentleman and smelled of something not quite pleasant, in fact he seemed to reek of garlic. Not his breath, he didn't say a word to her, but more as if his clothes had been saturated with it. Perhaps it was a determent for moths or other vermin that might inhabit trunks in foreign lands. She remembered hearing him say he was newly returned from the continent.

He noticed her attention and smiled, yellow teeth protruding from his walrus style mustache. "Your name is Jewel? Correct?" He traced his fingers down her arm to the top of her gloves, which thankfully reached to her elbow. "But not a jewel without a price." He laughed at his own joke. "I wonder if I have enough to lure you away from Mathews."

Miranda smiled widely, hoping the repulsion she felt didn't show on her face. "Oh, you do me such an honor, sir, but you must understand my loyalty is to Mr. Mathews. Without him, I wouldn't even be at such a place as this." True, but not in the same sense this man would take her answer to mean.

She was never so relieved as when the first course was set and she could turn to the man on her other side. The man she had wanted to speak with in the first place. The viscount turned to her and said something banal about the soup, and she nodded in agreement. Now how did one move from saying how tasty the soup was to ask whether he was a traitor? This spy business was trickier than it seemed.

She could see Morris sitting between the nippled woman and the host's mistress, both beautiful, both charming from a man's perspective. Why that should bother her, she wasn't sure. She was hoping he would be able to help her with her seating companion. She didn't actually care who was sitting next to him.

Morris met her gaze, and she knew he saw her and was giving what support he could offer so far from his side. She took strength in that and began, "I must confess I was lost when you gentlemen were talking politics before dinner. I mean it sounds so confusing and important, and you knew just how to explain your views."

The man preened as she hoped he would. "It is a very intricate and often delicate subject. Many men have differing opinions, and one would not wish to get into an argument at such a festive party as this. I usually refrain from stating my views so openly."

"Oh, I found it all so fascinating. I mean men have

such fascinating lives, don't you? It's just so, so—fascinating." She looked down at the man because he wasn't very tall even seated and smiled encouragingly. Trying to keep him talking.

She sent a glare that would kill toward the footman removing the soup plates and ended her conversation. She turned to the walrus as she ate her way through steamed salmon. She did quite well with always taking a forkful of fish just as the man asked another of his inappropriate questions. He kept trying to lure her away from Morris. First jokingly, but getting more and more lurid as she smiled, nodded, and yet unable to answer him because she was still chewing. How long could she fake chewing a bite of fish before even a man as single-minded as this one would catch on to her trick to ignore having to answer his suggestive remarks?

The next course arrived, and she took a sip of wine to make sure there wasn't time for the walrus to ask her any more indiscreet questions. Lord Wyngate was a welcome relief and seemed pleased to be conversing with her again as well. Perhaps the other woman was boring him. Whatever the reason, she was pleased she was given another private time to get his viewpoint on the royal family.

Realizing coming right out and asking would be a dead give-away to her inquisition, she let him choose the next subject, and hopefully she could find a way to lead him back to the politics of the day. Instead, he wanted to talk about his new carriage and four. How well they worked in harness and how matched they all were, even to the length of their stride. He was unsure as to whether to have their manes braided. She agreed she preferred to see horses' manes and tails blowing freely especially if

89

they were high steppers and speed was of the essence.

By the time the chicken in cream sauce was removed, she knew more than she wanted to about his horses and driver, but nothing new about his politics. As she turned back, her gaze met Morris' once again although neither acknowledged the other.

Without learning anything more about either of her companions' politics, Miranda stood when the other women left the men. Her last view of the dining room was of the footmen discreetly bringing in chamber pots for the male diners to use before their hour of bacchanal enjoyment of port and cigars.

Several of the women made use of the retiring room on the same floor before returning to the parlor where the group began the evening. The hostess was busy scribbling on pieces of paper torn from a single sheet. There were titters of laughter as several of the other women sat down next to her putting their heads close together.

Nipples entered and asked without much interest. "Another game? What's the difference? We'll have fucked them all by the end of the week either way."

The mistress-hostess looked up pouting. "This makes it more exciting. I mean this way we never know when we will get our special interest. Myself, I am looking forward to a little new meat. Mr. Mathews seems ripe for the picking, a lean and hungry look." The others all laughed then darted a glance at Miranda sitting by herself near the fireplace.

As they sought an answer, she shrugged her shoulders. "It is up to him who he sleeps with. I'm simply his guest at the moment."

The others accepted her remark and continued to

write.

When the men finally entered, Morris walked to stand behind her chair as the hostess stood up excitedly, the most animated Miranda had seen her all evening. "I have a game for everyone."

Her blue-eyed gaze moved around the room but stayed on Morris a second longer than the others. "You men select a question about one of the ladies present, and if you can guess which lady it refers to, you can take that lady to your room for the night."

That announcement brought titters from the woman and mild guffaws from the gentleman. Both Miranda and Morris remained silent.

Before the first note could be selected, Morris spoke up as he placed his hands on the top of Miranda's shoulders. "As sublime as that offer sounds, Jewel and I have made other plans. You will all have to excuse us. Although, I applaud your creative way of getting to know one another."

Morris helped Miranda stand and walked her out of the room to the groans of disappointment from both males and females alike.

Once in their room, Miranda turned to him and with heartfelt emotion. "Thank you for getting me away from those dreadful people. Are you sure any one of them has anything on their mind besides a weeklong orgy? I can't find a smidgeon of treason no matter how hard I look."

"You are not supposed to be looking. I need you here only as a cover for my being here. There is too much danger, and the man or men I'm seeking aren't going to blurt out their political ties to anarchists over *crème brûlée*."

"I understand. It is simply that I hate to waste time.

I am used to asking questions, and although I may have to sort the wheat from the chaff, the truth eventually shows itself."

He stared right in her eyes and said distinctly, "No wheat, no chaff, nothing. You will not involve yourself in my business at all."

"Yes, yes, if you say so, mighty master." She began to unpin and remove the brilliant hairpiece only for him to raise his hand to stop her.

"No, go ahead. That will work better for my plan."

She narrowed her eyes. "Plan? What plan?"

"I let it be known I planned on having sex with you in every one of the public areas in the house. There were a few bets placed that I cannot sustain such a feat given we have only one week, and there are forty such rooms." She felt her eyebrows rise. "I assured them I could do so easily, and if any of them were to come upon us, um, in *flagrant delicto* to please leave quietly."

"Why in the world would you say such a thing? I never gave you the slightest indication I would take part in such a, in such depravity." She was almost sputtering by the time she finished, stopping her mind from picturing him taking her on the long dining room table they were seated at less than two hours previously.

He watched her as if he were deciding something important, but then his expression changed and he smiled. "I told them that so when they find me, us, going through the various rooms where we have no right being, that we merely pretend to be finishing or starting copulation."

Now she did sputter. "B-beginning...f-f-finishing...what exactly...?"

"Nothing. We will be doing nothing. I will be

searching, and you can keep a lookout for anyone coming down the hall, et cetera. If we get caught, I may have to throw your skirt over your head and have my wicked way with you, but, after all, it's all for king and country."

She must have shown her shock because he laughed outright. "I'm sorry, Miranda, but I couldn't help myself. I will behave, I promise, and we will use the excuse that I am fulfilling the bet as we go from room to room."

He waved her to the door and peeked out. "They must still be playing the damn game. All is clear. I want to check out the office and library first. Two rooms usually devoted to hiding important papers and rarely used by houseguests."

Morris led the way, and she followed, tiptoeing although such silence was probably not needed. They didn't run into any staff, either. The benefit of such house parties was that staff was sparse and trained to stay out of the way unless given a direct decree by one of the guests.

They went back downstairs but turned away from the still noisy parlor. Evidently, the game included more than merely selecting a woman's name out of the bowl. Miranda tried to hide the shudder that took over her body as she thought of partnering with one of those other men—even for something as simple as dinner.

Morris led them down a dimly lit hall, only a few candle sconces glowed into the darkness proving this area little used in the evenings. He tried one doorknob which refused to budge. He got down on his knees in front of it and pushed in a piece of wire and voila, the knob turned and they were inside. But inside where? Miranda tried to make out the shapes of a large desk and high-backed Jacobean chairs, heavily carved with rope turned spindles. There was a rasp and then an oil lamp glowed on the desk.

Now Miranda could see everything. The heavy drapes at the two tall windows, the paintings depicting hunting scenes and horses. A cabinet behind the desk topped with ledger books of some kind. A leather couch and two wing chairs. She didn't know what should catch her eye as to appear out of place although she noted Morris didn't seem to have the same problem. He had already pried the desk drawers open and was riffling through them.

Looking up, he nodded his head toward the door. Miranda remembered her job and went to peek through the slit of the open door into the still darkened hall. She could hear Morris behind her, moving from the desk to the cabinet. She felt the moisture caused by the perspiration of her actions, her deception even if it were to strangers whom she owed no allegiance.

A muffled giggle preempted a couple stumbling around the corner, coming right at them. Miranda stifled the squeak of dismay and shut the door so the slim ray of light wouldn't be noticed in the dark hallway.

"Morris! Morris!" she said in a horse whisper as she hurried over to him. "Someone's coming. A couple, but they're heading this way. What do we do? Where do we hide?"

His head came up from under the desk. "We do as I said I would do. We have sex in one of the public rooms."

He pushed her backwards onto the couch and crashed down on top of her, covering her mouth with his as she began to argue about the need for such a display.

He kept his lips firmly to hers, his hand covering her breast and one leg between hers as she felt the coolness of the night air on her exposed stocking covered leg. There was no way to reach her skirts to pull them into some semblance of propriety and realized Morris didn't want her to look proper. He wanted her to look ravished.

The sound of the door opening was followed by giggles and a rough laugh. "Well, Stanhope better kiss his monkey good-bye. This was one room he thought Mathews wouldn't be able to breach, and here he is before us. Let's find a less populated room, my dear. This one seems to be taken." There was more laughter as the door closed, and Morris continued kissing her.

Miranda could see that the couple had left and ignoring his hand on her breast, pushed on his shoulder. "Morris, they're gone. You can get up now. I can see the room, and no one besides us is in here."

He continued to lie on her, his face now buried in the cleft of her bosoms. She could feel his hot breath coming in pants, and she thrust her hips up to push him off so she could pull down her skirts, but he couldn't be budged. She made the movement again.

"Miss Donner, if you do not stop wiggling, what I was merely imitating will become a fact. I did not take into consideration certain aspects of faking coitus and my body's responses. If you would spare me a moment longer, I think we will both be able to recover with our pride and virtue intact."

She stopped moving and tried to understand his words. She possessed a lot of experience, or the same experience repeatedly, of listening to women of the street relay what occurred between a man and a woman. She realized he had become aroused, but didn't that only happen when the man was interested? Or at least, preparing himself for intercourse? She didn't understand why he was getting prepared to have sex if that were not his intention. She refrained from thrusting up into his readied body and lay there waiting.

Finally putting one foot to the carpet, he pushed himself up and away from her. He brushed his fingers through his hair, and she thought she heard a huffed laugh of self-derision.

"Well, well, well. I learn something new every day."

She jumped at that piece of news. "You found something? In the cabinet?"

She could see him smile. "Not exactly, but I think we did all we could here. I was hoping since the room was kept locked it might contain something I could use." He put down his hand to help her to her feet as she tried to right her bodice and shake out her skirts.

"Why didn't you use your key to get in here? I saw you use something else."

He turned down the lamp and led her to the now closed door. "The key I have is for the housekeeper and only opens doors she needs access to like the bedrooms and main rooms. The steward's office and the master suites have a different key, which the butler and Stanhope carry."

He peered out and then pulled her along. "I think we can leave here although I'm afraid to search more tonight. I'd hate to run into Reynolds copulating in the butler's pantry."

The thought made her shudder as well, and she was happy to follow him back to their room.

They made it to their sleeping chamber without running into anyone including a servant. The parlor was

silent as well, which told her everyone had secured a
partner for the night and was attending to business or
whatever they referred to their having coitus as. Miranda
was never so thankful than she was to see the lamp still
lit next to the bed and her negligee, the one both the
modiste and Morris insisted she needed, laid out on the
open bed.

She looked longingly at the pristine white sheets. As
if he could read her mind, Morris spoke. "Go and get
ready for bed. I'll act lady's maid and help with your
strings, but then I'll leave you to your toilet. Perhaps a
short walk to smoke a cigar, and by the time I get back,
you'll be all tucked up in bed. Remember, you stick to
your side and I'll stick to mine."

Miranda wasn't sure when he returned because she
fell asleep so soundly, she never heard anything until
waking in the morning.

CHAPTER NINE

Morris was awake, shaved, and dressed for riding by the time Miranda opened her eyes. She looked over at the devilishly attractive man and groaned in frustration. "You appear perky as a sparrow while I know there will be dark circles under my eyes. How do men do that? Stay up and carouse and still appear as if they slept away the night peacefully?" She thought about her lack of clothing and remained under the covers.

"Well, I let you sleep for as long as I dared. Chased the maid away twice so I think you missed tea, but I'm sure we can get you something before luncheon."

"Luncheon? What time is it?"

"Hm-m-m. Almost noon. But I explained you were worn out from last night, and Reynolds confirmed it. He now says he will try to emulate me as well and make love in every room of the house. I evidently started a new trend, although I can't see that it will help my cause. I don't wish to trip over other couples every time I try to search a room."

She stayed where she was contemplating her choices.

"Just throw aside the covers. It's not like I haven't seen your delights before now."

"My...my delights? I've never been this bare in front of you. I wore my chemise, shift, and stockings."

"And lovely stockings they were with their pink

ribbon garters holding them in place."

"You remember the color of my garters?" she squeaked feeling it an accomplishment for making any form of an answer.

"Get out of bed, and I'll help with your corset and things. I know what I'm doing and won't make it so tight you can't breathe. Why women, especially woman such as you with a lovely figure, feel the need to lace yourself into this means of torture the inquisition would have salivated over, I cannot imagine."

He turned away from her, so she quickly made her way to the screen and washstand behind it to ready herself. He handed her pantaloons and a chemise behind the screen and then could hear him whistling as he moved about the room.

When she peeked out, there was a day dress laid out on the unmade bed.

He was busy fingering the jewelry he had brought with them. "I think this should do for this morning. The men are going to ride after lunch and look over a brook and pond Stanhope wants to see has fish."

"I shouldn't wear the riding habit?"

"No, that's for hunt day. None of the women were invited on this ride, nor will you be expected to get up at dawn and traipse down to the stream to cast for trout."

He tightened the corset to a perfectly comfortable size before dropping the dress over her head as if he were dressing a babe instead of a relatively attractive woman. Miranda wasn't sure why she felt piqued.

As she fixed her hair into a daytime style, she could see him in the background moving from his personal drawer. He unwrapped something, blew into it to expand it, and then spit and tossed it into the chamber pot. As he took a second, what he was doing dawned on her. She gasped and saw herself blush in the mirror.

He glanced up and caught her gaze. Laughing, he continued with the items. "I have to make it seem believable. I was thinking of leaving sex toys about but realized I have more sophistication than that. I'll just stick to the French letters. Three seem like the right number to you? If I had used more, you would get too sore since they're dipped in lye."

Miranda firmed her lips not wanting to display any form of feminine annoyance at the outrageous things he was saying. "I know all about such things and have no opinion of how many or how often you wish to throw them about the room."

His eyes were glittering with suppressed humor as he continued to hold her gaze reflected in the looking glass. Finally, he seemed content with his props and smiling, actually waved as he left her to finish her toilet.

She approached the morning dining room used for breakfast and luncheon according to a passing footman to find half the women missing. The mistress-hostess was present, and she smiled a welcome.

"Jewel, come sit by me and let's get to know one another. I hope what I said last night about Mr. Mathews didn't put you in a bad mood. I meant no harm. After all, I am well ensconced in Lord Stanhope's life. Although it is a precarious position, I feel he is as strong a man as I need. I will not poach."

A footman brought her a plate of selections from the buffet set out since this was an informal meal with only some of the guests awake even at noontime.

Miranda understood this type of woman. Caro knew where she stood and how delicate the line she walked.

Much like the tightrope-walkers Miranda marveled over at the circus.

"I took no offense. Like you, I know I have little control of the man in my life. He may be with me no longer than this house party no matter how I may wish it otherwise."

"I don't think you have to worry so much in that vein. I watched him with you last night, and he was a man staking his claim, warning the others to back away. It may change later in your relationship, but not very soon. I know when a man is interested in a woman, and he is still interested in you. Very much so. He ignores any bait the others have thrown out to him."

Not sure of what to say, how much to pretend to be like this woman and still not be caught in a lie, Miranda smiled and agreed. "Well, it is early days yet. I feel lucky to have found a protector so trustworthy. I know I could have done a lot worse."

The other woman rolled her eyes. "Even here, there are men I try to miss being near, but Lord Stanhope has a reputation as a gracious host. Everything a guest wants that is within Stanhope's reach to provide, he will. He hates to be thought of as less than generous." A sadness passed over the older woman.

Miranda knew at that moment, more than any other, how difficult these women's lives were, how tenuous their grasp of fortune which could turn on a penny. Could the woman mean anything besides sharing her with other men?

"You are a beautiful woman. You could find a stingier protector. One who is selfish and wants to keep you to himself."

A far-off dreamy expression appeared on her as yet

unlined face. "That would be nice again. Just the two of us. It all changed when he became friends with Sir Thomas and Lord Wyngate. Now it's house party after house party, and I am no longer considered private goods." A tear rolled down Caro's cheek quickly absorbed by a napkin.

"I am sorry." And Miranda was. She had been dealing with women like the one in front of her for years now, and each time their story broke her heart, made her weep with guilt she was so blessed to have her aunt and her career such that it was. This woman would be old and broken before she was thirty. "Is there anything I can do to help?"

The mistress-hostess took her at her word, unerringly knowing Miranda could be trusted. "No, I don't think so, but I thank you for your kind offer. Lord Stanhope said this should be over soon. That this would be the last house party. I would no longer have to…entertain these men again."

Miranda thought about the woman's confession. "So, Mr. Mathews will no longer be invited to a country party such as this?"

"Not by Lord Stanhope. He told me we would go and possibly live on the continent, perhaps France now that the war is over. He said by this time next month we would be able to travel freely wherever we want. He would be free to leave his wife who is related to the king. So far, it has been difficult for him to live life as he has wanted."

"Oh, I did not realize Lord Stanhope was so well situated."

"He doesn't want to be and has said his life would have been much easier if he hadn't married the king's cousin's daughter, but he did so under pressure. She was not attractive, had over indulged in biscuits in the schoolroom, and went to fat and pimples. It is said she even resembles the king, but what is acceptable in a man is not attractive in a woman. Lord Stanhope has had a cross to bear although, it seems, he won't have to carry it much longer."

The woman sat more erect and smiled a welcome. "Oh, here is Collette. Darling, come tell me about your new mantua maker. I loved that gown you wore last evening."

Miranda went to find a quiet place to contemplate this new piece of information. She didn't think she would find out any more about Lord Stanhope and his plans to leave England perhaps after a coup. With Collette's arrival, the women would talk about fashion, and Miranda needed to think. What exactly did it mean, if anything, for Morris?

Walking towards the conservatory, she was anxious to search more rooms but knew she didn't have any idea what would help him and what wouldn't. She paused before opening the door, finding the temperature inside several degrees warmer and the air moist and redolent with the odors of moss and soil. A stone bench invited her, and she moved to it, astounded by the abundance of flowers and ferns in pots and planters surrounding her. Some even overhanging and climbing the metal and glass enclosure.

"Well, well, well, who do we have here? Miss Jewel, isn't it?" Sir Thomas stepped out from behind a large palm frond.

Miranda jumped and then laughed holding her hands close to her chest. "Oh, Sir Thomas, you startled me. I thought I was the only one taking in the scents and beauty of the flowers." She dropped her hands and relaxed.

"I'm sure you could have thought of some other way to meet me in private. A woman of your charms and abilities must know many tricks of the trade." He stepped closer and blocked her path of retreat.

She became nervous of his soft words and tried to remember how to flirt her way out of a predicament. Too late, she remembered the first rule was not to get into such a predicament in the first place. She threw out a red-herring. "I thought all the men had gone out to look at some fish or something."

"Some did and some didn't. I'm not much of a fisherman. Too little action." His gaze roamed her body in a predatory manner. "If I want something to fight my line, I want it to be worth capturing."

"Capturing. An unusual choice of words for fishing."

"We are not talking about fishing here, and you know it. I like a little play though. Are you going to try to escape before I can get my kiss, or are you going to stand there and accept my dominance? Because that's what a kiss is. Dominance—it is someone taking over control of another's body whether by tying them up and forcing them to endure their touch, their kisses, their entrance or accepting the other's control."

"I, I don't believe Mr. Mathews would like me here with you at all. I think you should let me go, allow me to pass." She tried to keep her head up, not allow him to control her through her fears.

"You think too much for a woman. That is what men are for. We will tell you how to dress, how to act, and what to think. The English are weak from having been controlled by queens in the past. They should have learned that only men, real men of strength, should rule the nation, hold the crown."

Feeling in need to make him concentrate on something other than keeping her trapped, she lashed out, "That sounds almost like sedition."

His eyes darkened as he snarled, "I knew you were too smart for your own good. Get over here and tell me what you know of such things." He tugged on her arm, yanking her to the stonewall of the house where they could not be seen through the glass doors. He pressed her up against the damp blocks, his hips holding the lower portion of her body in place. "Now we will see who is dominant. I take it you do not want to kiss me, that you do not want to fuck me." He ground his hips into hers as she felt his arousal bruising her pelvic bone.

Fear flooded her body; she wanted to shove him, but he was stronger, and he took glee in her puny efforts to thwart him. She didn't have her gun with her. Had never thought to load it and carry it around with her in the house. Morris never thought she would be endangered. She knew he hadn't, or he would never have left her alone. She tried to think of anything the prostitutes told her about protecting herself, but that was for men who were attacking. This one already had much of her body under his control through brute strength.

"Mr. Mathews, Morris, will take issue with your treatment of me, I assure you. He promised me I would not be abused while under this roof."

"Well, Mathews should not have left you alone after making that announcement he would be the only one allowed to tup you. Then bragging he would take you in every public room of the house. So how many times has that been so far? Five? Ten? If it were me, I would be through the common rooms and on to the sleeping quarters taking you along with any other woman there."

She was truly frightened the man seemed to be feeding his own lusts. "I don't want to be here. Let me go, and I won't tell Morris what has happened."

He squeezed her upper arms tighter and snarled, "We have already discussed how what you want does not matter. I am dominant…"

And the man was gone. She opened her eyes to see Morris, his face red with anger as he punched Sir Thomas with two fast jabs to the nose and then one to his stomach when the knight put his hands up to protect his face.

Sir Thomas tried to stand and take a fighter's stance but staggered backward as Morris repeated the one-two and punch to the gut—this time followed by an upper cut with his right fist. The knight fell to his knees and then onto his face in the floor now puddled with bloody water.

Morris turned to her, his anger still apparent on his face and his stance. He grabbed her, hauled her out of the conservatory and down the hall towards the front of the house. Miranda stumbled then dug in her heels knowing how her tear-streaked face and torn dress would cause a stir.

"No, not that way."

Something must have seeped through to him, and he turned toward the servants' stairs pulling her up with him, not letting go of her until they were in their room and the door slammed shut.

CHAPTER TEN

Morris stared at her. The once lovely dress smeared with mud and moss. Her sleeve torn and the bodice covered with smudges. There were signs of tears having run down her face, but her eyes were dry now. He wanted to rant and rave and kill someone.

"What the hell do you think you were doing in a room away from everyone else with a man like that? Did you think you could get him to incriminate himself when I couldn't? Do you think talking with a bunch of broken prostitutes makes you qualified to handle an assignment like this?"

She stared at him from frightened eyes, her body trembling. He became so angry he couldn't stop his lashing out at her for endangering herself. Thinking what could have happened if he had stayed with the group as they rode on to the pond after checking the stream. He had almost remained with them thinking the ride was possibly an assignation, but with most of them going, he realized they wouldn't meet anyone as a group. Only one or two of them are involved, and the rest merely used to cover up any clandestine meetings.

"I never should have brought you. I trusted you to do as I told you and stay out of trouble, away from danger. Now I must explain why I beat up one of my host's guests. Left him in a pile of his own blood and vomit. Would you like to tell me what you thought you were doing?"

She appeared so lost, so fragile with her eyes dark pools of pain and betrayal. Yes, that's what he saw—betrayal. Why did she think he owed her anything after what she had done? To meet with a man whether or not he was an anarchist was dangerous to a lone woman. A man who had shown his baser desires and tendencies by simply attending this house party in the first place.

"Get cleaned up. We will have hell to pay for today's business. I should send you back to Soho. Stay and take my pleasure with women who know their place in this world, know how to listen to a man, know how to please a man."

Disgusted with himself, he heard her sobs, angry that he couldn't find the compassion to stop and console her. After all, she had come close to being raped, and she knew it. He knew he should be comforting her not yelling at her like a brute, but his emotions were too raw, too close to the surface. He feared that if he touched her, he would traumatize her just as much.

He left the room not wanting to take advantage of her in this fragile state. Didn't want her to cling to him because he saved her from a fate worse than death when in truth she would never have been in that position if it hadn't been for him in the first place. Would have never been endangered, never been anywhere near a man like Thomas.

It was all his fault.

She would never, should never have been here. She possessed no skills or training to deal with men of Thomas' ilk even if she wanted to uncover the conspiracy to overthrow the crown and government of England. She was practical and she thought worldly, but in fact, she knew very little of the real world. Yes, he must admit she knew more than she should about some things, but that did not make her qualified for attending this house party.

His mistake was to think that he could protect her as well as do his assignment. He had been wrong. She was too attractive to be left alone at this type of a house party, too willing to help him in any way she could. He should never have brought her. Should have sent her home when he saw the envy and avarice in the other men's eyes as they met her. But he was weak and wanted her to be his if even for a week, if even only in a peripheral way.

Miranda was someone who was too good for him, too kind and gentle for him. He wasn't worth her, an intelligent woman, a woman who knew what she wanted and had found a way to get it. She did nothing besides try to help others—her aunt, the streetwalkers, and even the medical student. Her thoughts were always for others. Even coming with him here. He knew she didn't do it for the money or dresses. She wanted to make a difference and help keep the royals safe.

He should have cleared her name with Whitehall and found another way to get to his potential seditionists. He should have been here with her. This was his fault, and he needed to go back and apologize. Beg her to forgive his failure to think about her being left in the house when he knew men were missing from the outing.

Perhaps that was what had been niggling at the back of his mind while he was riding. He didn't like the idea of not knowing where Thomas and Wyngate had gotten to, but they weren't with the rest of the male guests. Possibly that was why as soon as he reached the house he went in search of Miranda, worried when he found the other women in the card room playing loo. The hostess told him she hadn't seen Jewel since luncheon. Then he had found her in that beast's arms, her cries to be let lose ringing against the glass roof.

Morris got his emotions under control and his rational thoughts turned to helping Miranda rather than accuse her for disobeying him. He opened the door to his room, expecting to see Miranda prostrate on the bed, perhaps still sobbing over his treatment of her. Instead, he found the room warm and redolent with the fragrance of violets and vanilla, a scent he always associated with her. She had closed the drapes and lit a candle, which sat on the table by the bed.

Miranda was lying in a tub, her hair pinned up with tendrils floating as she rested her head against the curved back. She didn't move, and he thought she was possibly sleeping although he very much wanted to see her. Teasingly she had left bare parts of her smooth skin showing. Her perfectly porcelain shoulders, the expanse of bosom with its tantalizing cleavage which he had the chance one time of burying his face into and breathing in her essence.

She was sleeping. A trail of tears still showed on her cheeks, and he wanted to kiss them away, show her she hadn't done anything wrong. Show her he was upset with himself for ever putting her in danger. After berating her for not protecting herself better in Whitechapel, he had left her in a house with randy potential insurgents. He needed to protect her and still find the men he was pursuing.

He moved closer. The bruises, which had not shown before, had time to come to the surface, forming blue marks the size of a man's hands on her upper arms, her shoulder, even one on her breasts. He cursed under his breath. It must have been loud enough to wake her.

She splashed water over the sides as she sat straighter and realized she was no longer alone, that he was there and standing quite near. She put her hands up trying to cover her nudity and doing an insufficient job. He brought her a towel and laid it across her upper torso.

"You're back," she said needlessly although her words broke the silence between them.

"I owe you an apology. I raked you over the coals when I had no reason to do so. I left you alone with a possible traitor, and it is my duty to protect you."

She gazed up, her lip trembling. "I didn't go after him. I didn't know he was there. I didn't have anything in common with the other women and thought I should stay aloof unless they found out. I thought it would be a good place to sit and wait for you to return so we could go through more rooms."

"He was already there? Did you think it odd?"

"Yes, but he began saying things like I should leave you and be with him. That he would know what to do with me. Then he pushed me up against the wall, and I couldn't get away." Her voice broke, and there were tears again. "It's not like when someone tells you to fight off an attacker. A man's strength is much scarier when he uses it against you. I would not have gotten away if you hadn't arrived."

He knelt next to the tub ignoring the water as it wetted his breeches. "Shush-shush, but I did arrive. I must make sure you are safely by my side at all times from now on. I must continue the search, but we will continue as we planned. The two of us."

He brushed the tendrils of hair back from her

feverish forehead. "Am I forgiven? I never meant to make you feel guilty. It was my over-reaction to you being in danger. I arrived in time, and Thomas will not bother you again. I can guarantee that."

"I'm sorry I got in trouble and was the reason you beat up one of the potential criminals you are after."

"Well, he'll put down the beating as a sign of me being a jealous lover. I already gave fair warning for all of the men to leave you alone. That you and I were still too new for any form of sharing."

"If you think it won't cause you to be kicked out of the house party, I'll stay."

His heart lightened. She was still his. "I would have to leave if you did since I wouldn't have my own woman. Even if I don't partake of someone else's, it would seem I would be a distraction, actually an oddity to stay on."

"I didn't think of that. I thought you would want me gone. You were so angry at me."

"Not at you, at myself although you bore the brunt of my wicked disposition. Are you done in there? I want to see to those bruises. I have an ointment that may help and a powder you should mix with water to ease the pain. If I realized he had hurt you like this, I wouldn't have stopped hitting him when I did."

She gave him a tentative smile. "I think he will remember not to touch me next time. And besides, if you put him into bed to recuperate you might never find the man or men you've been hunting."

He helped her stand. Water ran down her limbs as he wrapped a dry bath sheet around her. He patted her body gently, treating her injuries with careful attention, not allowing his body to react to hers. Her naked skin, her clean fresh scent, her vulnerability as she leaned into him and used his strength as her own.

Laying her on the bed, he covered her just as she was.

"Rest for a while and if you feel like it, then you can come down to dinner. If not, we'll look through a few more rooms yet tonight. My luck that it happened to be one of the grander houses that has so many rooms even the staff have forgotten some of them."

She nodded, her eyes closing already. He stood over her wishing he had done things differently that afternoon. Either stayed with her or ordered her to stay in her room. Anything to keep her safe from the likes if the men at this party. Although the country house only held men of the *ton*, men who were allowed within the confines of the royal rooms and government buildings, he should have been more watchful. He was seeking an insurgent without scruples. Any form of terrorism could be used to disrupt and prevent the government's normal ability to run the nation and protect the people from the ravages of a violent overthrow of the present government. His attention could not be divided. He must focus on finding the danger to his king and England's security as a nation.

****

A well-rested Miranda, wearing the turquoise gown shot with silver, finished dressing for dinner. She wore strands of fine silver woven through her hair and dusted her face with rice powder before tinting her lips as Morris' maid had taught her.

"You don't need that you know," Morris said as he walked in from the dressing room freshly shaved by the valet all the men shared.

"Your maid, Sally, told me to use it. It's to make me

appear as the other women…"

He stepped quickly up behind her and covered her mouth with a finger, appearing as if he was kissing her neck in a prelude to making love.

"No, you're right. Now is not the time to have to re-do your toilet. I can wait for another hour or two." In her ear, he whispered, "There is someone watching us. Do not say anything."

Staring at her reflection in the mirror, she didn't change her actions, adding one more swipe of the narrow brush to her full lower lip. He could not believe he hadn't heard anyone listening and watching them before. He had done a cursory search for any secret panel, but the owner of the house never mentioned one nor did the missive sent to his superior in the government.

When she went to put on her earbobs, he pressed her hand gently, and she released the silver items, her gaze meeting his in the mirror with unanswered questions.

"You're so beautiful. I am the luckiest man here tonight."

She smiled although seemed unsure of what he wanted from her. He leaned down and kissed her lips again as she held her face up, accepting his salute. He found he didn't want to stop and almost forgot there was someone watching, that he had begun this as a ruse to fool whoever it was into believing they were a couple involved in themselves.

"Let us go down for dinner, the first gong went off a few moments ago."

"Did it?" she asked honestly. He knew she was confused by his kiss and unsure of what was an act and what he really meant. He was suffering from the same distraction.

She reached for a shawl shot with silver thread. "I need this to cover my arms."

He didn't need a reminder since the bruising was noticeable. He bent and kissed those as well.

Once in the parlor, they were surrounded by the others. He was speaking with the men, most coming up to congratulate him for putting Sir Thomas in his rightful place. He turned to look at Miranda.

"Jewel, you've forgotten your earbobs. Let me get them for you since I think I was the reason you became distracted while you dressed." He allowed a secret message sent and received as the others watched enviously.

He left the room knowing she would be safe with all the others in attendance.

Morris touched and pressed along every piece of trim and molding he could find. No secret passage opened into his room anywhere near where he knew he heard the noise. He was sure it had been something like a scrape although he couldn't find any marks on the polished wood floorboards surrounding the Aubusson carpet.

Sitting where Miranda had been at the mirror, he watched his reflection. He searched the background and then stood quickly, turning and walking to the heavy full-length clothes press. Getting down on his knees, he felt the floorboards beneath the heavily carved behemoth piece of furniture. There it was. He rubbed the flat of his hand over the same spot and felt the raised edge of a cutout rectangle. He pried with his nail and finally got one side to release, and it telescoped from the floor, a mirror showed and reflected the bed back to itself.

So, Stanhope or someone liked to watch. The

Peeping Tom could stand or sit in the safety of a room one floor below and watch what occurred on the bed in this room. Well, if they were watching, it would have been a boring show. That would not mean he and Miranda hadn't blessed each of the other rooms in the house with their copulations and once back to their own bed were too drained to partake again.

He had the feeling though that his beating Thomas had brought about the interest. Someone wasn't as convinced that he and Miranda were a couple or he, or she, wanted to see what kind of relationship the two had. Blackmail could be a motive with less information. Anyone who knew him knew he often worked for men high in the government. Perhaps someone wanted to use information against him or coerce him into working for the other side.

Needing to return to the others before they went in to dinner, he pushed the section closed and patted it as flat as he could although no one would find it under normal conditions. He stood up, dusting the knees of his breeches off making sure there were no smudges and grabbed the silver earbobs as he passed the dressing table.

He arrived just as the butler announced dinner and escorted Miranda into the dining room. Walking around the table, he found her place card, then lifting it, replaced it with the one of the women sitting next to him. He smiled as he then sat Miranda in the chair. Stanhope's hostess didn't make a peep of complaint at the high-handedness of moving her place settings. The woman he moved seemed a little disappointed but then shrugged and smiled serenely at the man who was now her table companion.

Sitting when the rest of the men did, he took Miranda's hand, raising it to his lips, and kissed the knuckles. She blushed smiling sweetly but did not pull away. Evidently willing to play whatever game he required of her. The thought reared its head at the same time his body responded to her scent. He was going to enjoy this dinner as much as others might find it uncomfortable. No one mentioned the empty chair at the end of the table. Thomas must not feel up to chewing his meal, and Morris couldn't feel a bit sorry for the man.

The footmen brought around the first course, and Morris remained quietly talking with Miranda, whispering in her ear and leaning over to place small nipping kisses on her neck. Her little sighs and giggles as he tickled her neck with his warm breath made his heart swell. This playing at being the jealous lover was turning into a lot of fun. He should have thought of it sooner.

When the second course arrived and Miranda should have turned to the man to the other side of her, the Viscount Reynolds, Morris wouldn't let her do so. She tried to object to his keeping her full attention on him, but he refused to yield the field, and she remained facing him, allowing him liberties with her shoulder and neck. He also took his fill of gazing at her cleavage, but, at least, held himself back from licking or caressing her there. Besides, there was still time yet. It was only the third course.

He noticed the table was altogether quieter, many watching his antics and placing discreet bets as to whether he and his Jewel would make it through the entire meal or not. This amused him so much he almost knocked the plate of breaded pork chops out of the footman's hands when he came to serve him. The true amusement in Miranda's eyes was worth the minor embarrassment of seeming so smitten with his mistress he was head over heels.

He was sure most of the others at the table were ready to write a note to the more notorious newspapers to tell them this informational tidbit. He almost laughed aloud when he thought what his superior would think of it when he saw it in print. Probably nominate Morris for a medal for going beyond the call of duty. That was only because the man had never met Miranda.

When the women stood to leave the men to their port, Morris stood as well pulling Miranda toward the doorway. "Gentleman, I will see you in the morning, um, the late morning. My companion and I are out and about the house once again." He laughed and rushed Miranda out before she could protest as the hoots and banter from his fellow guests followed them.

CHAPTER ELEVEN

They moved quietly after the catcalls died off. Morris knew there was one room he needed to explore before he found any other. He wanted to find that special room under their sleeping chamber. Turning down first one hall and then another, winding his way through the passages until he found a door to the room that would be beneath his own.

Pulling on the knob, he found it locked, then used the key that should have opened all bedrooms, but it didn't open it either. Pulling out the little leather case of metal wires, he inserted two and the door snicked opened. Stepping in, he pulled Miranda with him. He wasn't going to leave her where one of the men might opportune her, not again.

The room was dark as night, but Morris was prepared for such an event. He pulled out the candle he brought, handing it to Miranda. The sound of a flint, the welcome spark and the flame built-up to full brightness. Taking the candle, he held it above his head in front of them. They were in a room with a chair on a raised dais. He could see the mechanism that controlled the trap door and the mirrors that reflected the events occurring on the bed. There didn't seem to be anything more.

He checked for any changes in air current, any light showing around a secret panel, and any scrapes on the floor to indicate a wall swung open. He found one of those. Feeling around the edge of the wall and tapping gently he was finally rewarded by the creak of a seldom used door opening into a cobweb covered passageway. He held the candle up in both directions.

"Unless someone crawled on his hands and knees through here, it's been left to the spiders and mice. At one time, it was probably used as a priest's hole. I can't say I'm not disappointed in finding this empty. If it had been used, then we would have to consider all the guests a possibility. There should be just one person who knows about this room, but it may not be our host. That mirror pops up in our room and focuses on our bed."

Her eyes opened wide. She stared at the chair and then the mirror system, and her mouth formed a big O as the realization hit her. "I was in my bath. Do you think I was watched?"

Morris didn't hesitate to lie. "No, I'm sure if anyone watched it was to see what I was doing. I mean, I've been the one under scrutiny. I never did figure out how I got on the guest list for this party. I hadn't even found the right house until the invitation fell into my lap."

She peered around the mostly empty room. "Well, I can see this isn't going to help you find the men you need to find. Where should we go next?"

He smiled, amazed at how much she wanted to help him even after everything that had happened to her. Holding out his hand, she grasped it as he said, "Come on, no one expects to see us for hours. Probably not till tomorrow morning."

She led him out the door this time, turning to him for direction. He pointed her toward the servants' stairs. "I still haven't seen the library, so that's next on my list. There was always too much activity during the day for me to get in there, and no one would believe I wanted a book to read to put me to sleep." Her expression of shock at his teasing made him chuckle.

"So, let's check there first and then try another and another until we run out of rooms," she told him enthusiastically as she began hastening toward the stairs that would take them to the ground floor.

Morris blew out the candle as he followed her, astounded at how game she was to help him find the men endangering their king.

The library was much easier to find, located behind the formal parlors with doors onto the garden. He opened the door using his set of tools, and they slid into the dark room. Relocking it behind them, each took a lamp and searched through the shelves.

"Morris, what should I be looking for?" She stood in front of a bookcase perusing the titles of the books lining the shelves.

"Any anomalies. Anything that looks like it doesn't belong or hasn't been here very long. The upper shelves that are dust covered we won't need to examine too deeply. It has to be something that can be retrieved easily as well."

She nodded then methodically began perusing the lower shelves. Ones that would get the most activity and cleaning. Anything higher than her head were dust covered with the books fitted tightly together in their confined space.

"No luck for you either?" Morris asked quietly from the desk.

"No, this may take all night."

They stopped talking when a key scraped in the lock. Morris gazed at Miranda, her eyes large with fear and scrambled from where he was to her side.

"Lean against the shelves and act like you're in ecstasy."

"What…?" Before she could say anything, ask anything, he dove beneath her dress and hugged her hips, leaning his face against her mound.

Through the gossamer fabric, Morris could see Lord Stanhope standing in the doorway framed by the hall lights behind him. The key was still in his hand as he stared at the couple silhouetted in the candles' glow.

"Damn, you're good Mathews. How you get into these rooms is beyond me, but you just may break me if I must pay off my wagers to those other two. I would have sworn a man couldn't accomplish what you said you'd do. Oh, pardon me, Jewel." Leaning down he called out a little louder, "My apologies, Mr. Mathews. I'll see you both in the morning." Stanhope backed out and closed the door.

Morris felt Miranda expel the breath she had held as her heartbeats returned to normal. He wanted to remain where he was with his arms around her hips, his mouth near her most intimate spot, and his heart beating to the rhythm of hers.

He gave a quick kiss on her thigh, then rocked back on his heels and came out from under her skirt. He looked up at the loveliest thing he had ever seen. She was bright pink, her eyes shining in the candles' light and mortification written all over her face.

"Don't be embarrassed, Miranda. You have saved my bacon once again. What other excuse could I have devised which so accurately makes the person who belongs here apologize for interrupting? Finding a couple in a compromising position makes others feel that if I had any other choice, I would not be caught making love."

"I understand. It's just that I wasn't expecting what you did, and I was caught off guard. I was surprised is all. I've written about such things after all." She adjusted her skirts and then the bodice of her dress, patting her hair for good measure.

"I'm not sure it's in this room either. Stanhope certainly didn't seem agitated to find us in here, merely surprised." He peered around seeing nothing unusual.

"Um, while I was pressed against the shelves, I noticed something I hadn't seen in the dim lamp light. With light from the hall shining across that paneling, I saw a lighter square around the oil painting hanging there. I think the one there now replaced a larger painting that had protected the paneling from the smoke from the chimney. The smaller painting is new."

"Really? What is the painting of?" He strode across the room and studied the painting in question, wiping his fingers gingerly over the dark then lighter wood. "It's of the Tower of London. Not badly done although I don't recognize the artist. Do you think it would be that obvious?"

Miranda shrugged looking at him expectantly. "Maybe it's in some kind of code. Are there numbers or letters within the context of the picture? Like the number of bricks times the height of the wall around the compound?"

"You're trying too hard." He studied the painting bringing one of the lamps closer to where it shown upon the artwork itself. He took the painting down and examined the back, checking the canvas for any markings or hidden sections. "Here it is, along the inside where the canvas has been folded over and tacked down. Sometimes on a small piece as this one, this area is painted. Instead, this canvas is bare and there are pencil markings. I think it indicates a date - yes, it's dated for two weeks from today."

"You don't think Lord Stanhope was here to see this, do you?"

"Why would he need to wait until the middle of the night while a woman probably waits in his bed? He could come in here anytime, and he wouldn't need a house party as an excuse to do so."

"Could it be the house party is a way to get various people under one roof, one to leave a message for another and neither of them knowing who that other person is?"

He paused for a moment. "You may have something there. If no one knows who the other is, then both would be careful not to give themselves away. Moreover, there is no way to tell who the two are either. Only that they are of the eight."

"Well, you can count yourself out, but I wouldn't leave the women off the list. There have been women who have carried messages during times of war throughout history."

"All right, now you've doubled the number leaving you and me out of the equation. You've given me a big job. We won't know if the intended spy has already seen the painting or not. If we take it down the one who hung it will know, and if we leave it up, the one who needs to find it will get the information."

"Change the message."

"Wha…? Of course, I'll simply change the date forward so if the person the message is intended for hasn't seen it yet they will be at London Tower early and we can capture him. If not, then we must do it the old fashion way and catch them in the act of sedition. We will, of course, make sure none of the royal family is anywhere near the public or Tower of London around the date written on the back of this painting."

"I agree that sounds like the best plan. Am I to be one of the 'we'?"

He raised one brow in answer as he crossed the room and returned from a small secretary with a pencil. He changed the date easily enough and rehung the painting, making sure it appeared just as he found it. They left the room, locking the door behind them.

Bringing her back to their room, he looked over to the clothing press to make sure the hidden trap wasn't open. "I'll help you get out of your dress and then go for a stroll. I want to see where everyone is at this moment."

"Don't bother to tell me the details. I have enough knowledge and would rather be able to look these women in the eye over luncheon."

Laughing, he untied the corset. "I would rather not know some of the things I have to see as well. Hopefully these people are rather tame in their tastes."

****

Miranda snuggled under the sheets, the flimsy negligée giving little warmth. Her cheeks heated remembering those few wonderful minutes in the library as Morris hugged her hips. She felt his warm breaths on her thighs and worried he would do something audacious while she wouldn't be able to stop him. Like the time in the office, she wondered if he was also becoming aroused, passion flaming into life.

She had tried to remember to appear as if she were

in the throes of an ecstatic episode for their audience. At the same time, once the door shut, she wanted Morris to continue his distraction. Her curiosity was heated, and the lick of desire warmed her ardor.

She never thought such propinquity would make her want to throw off her lifetime of proper living. Other than her writing pursuits, she led an exemplary life. She attended church without feeling she had committed a sin, even in her thoughts. Now, Morris was tempting her to leave all her better principles behind.

Morris was showing her what she had only heard about before. His touch, his warm breath, and his smoldering gaze made her heart flutter in anticipation. Dinner tasted like sawdust under his attention. All she wanted was for him to grab her and carry her to this room, to this bed. His hot stares made her feel powerful, made her want to plead for him to taste the skin his gaze returned to over and over again.

When he pulled her out of the dining room in full view of everyone, she would have gone readily to this room with him. Take one of those packets holding the French letter and offer up her virginity to him, mirror in the floor or not.

Yawning, she tried staying awake until he returned. Would she have the nerve to tell him how much her thinking had changed since being at the house party with him? Explain that his offer might be just the type of arrangement she would be interested in?

****

When Morris returned, Miranda was curled up in the bed sound asleep. He undressed and crawled in his side, wishing they were in bed for other reasons than because he was on assignment. He listened to her soft breathing until he fell asleep as well.

She woke him by snuggling into his bare chest, whimpers like a kitten mewing clawed at his heart.

He whispered, not wanting to startle her. "Miranda, Miranda wake-up. You're having a nightmare. Everything is alright."

His words finally got through to her. "Oh, Morris, it was horrible. Sir Thomas had me trapped and I c-couldn't get away and I...I couldn't find you." A hiccup sob escaped, and he felt a tremor ripple through her.

His arm tightened automatically. "I'm here now, and he is not going to repeat what he tried before, believe me. Try to sleep and forget him. He isn't worth it."

Silently she lay in his arms, twirling her fingers in his chest hair. A rather pleasant feeling. His body began to respond to her touch, her nearness. He needed to remember why she was there. That she would have been safe in her own bed if it hadn't been for his refusal to believe she was innocent.

"It was only a dream. Now go to sleep, and we'll talk about it in the morning if you want." He began to pull his arm from beneath her.

"I don't think I can keep doing what I have been doing. Not after yesterday," she said quietly barely above a whisper.

"I think I'm done here. We can tell our host the incident over Thomas has made me change my mind about staying."

"Not this, I can stay here as long as I know where you are, in case I need you. What I'm worried about is later. I don't think I can go back to Whitechapel again. What if a man like Sir Thomas catches me, and I can't get to my flintlock, shoot him before he, before he...?"

"Don't think that way, Miranda. You would have thought of something if I hadn't shown up. I'm sure you would have."

"But he was so brutal and angry, saying all kinds of vile things." She buried her face into his chest, her breaths rustling over his heated skin.

Bringing his hand up to push her away, he brushed her breast. She leaned into it, and he could feel the nipple firm immediately. He left his hand cupped over the soft orb knowing what he was doing was something he would regret later, but too late to prevent what he was going to allow to happen tonight.

****

Miranda found Morris' warm palm a solace to her body as it sought closeness to his. She wanted to push today's memories to the back of her mind, wanted to cover it with a more pleasant one. His hand over her breast, the way his thumb rubbed the nipple seemed to be one way to forget.

Flattening her hand, she covered his breast wondering if he would like it, too. He seemed to. His breath hitched. His nipple pebbled beneath her feather-light touch. She leaned in and nuzzled then kissed the soft fur covering much of his chest. This time he rewarded her with a soft kiss, a homage of sorts.

Wanting more, she pushed closer, urging him to touch her. Wanting to feel what a woman feels when a man caresses her. She didn't doubt Morris cared for her, would make love to her if she gave him enough encouragement. She wanted to know how making love felt, a man she cared about touching her in the most intimate of ways.

If she had experienced that already, would what Sir

Thomas had done yesterday have affected her so strongly? Would she be able to face fighting off an attacker if she once knew love as it was meant to be?

Feeling his tongue rub across her bottom lip, she opened instinctively knowing that's what he wanted of her. He swooped in as soon as she did, and a feeling of something urgent rushed through her body. She wanted to make him feel the same way and slipped her tongue against his, the response caused him to pull her closer. Now she could feel his arousal. He must be naked, and her fine muslin gown was no protection between them.

He deepened the kiss while stroking her body from hip to breast. His other hand held her hips tightly to his. He pressed against her even as he rucked the bottom of the gown up, exposing her hair covered mound. It was as if she had died and gone to heaven when he cupped the heated area, a slight pressure to reassure her that he wasn't leaving soon.

Stretching her neck, she gave him access to the soft skin there. He licked and sucked below her ear before returning to her mouth. His hand remained unmoving until he lowered his head and suckled a firmed nipple. She arched with the pleasure, trying to ensure he didn't leave her. Not like this. Not until he satisfied the need, this desire swirling through her body.

Miranda wanted to give him everything. Wanted to feel everything. To feel him in her, on her, pressing his hot erection into her. She wanted to know what it was to be a woman with the man she loved.

No, not loved, she could not love this man, any man. She needed to remain a writer, but that didn't preclude her making love. More research, more knowledge. That was all this was, all it ever could be. She had made her decision years ago, and she had no regrets. Not when it led to this night, this man and where she knew this was heading.

Pushing her hips toward him once more, he increased his suckling as he slid a finger into her. He felt cool to her passion-heated skin, the silkiness unknown to her as he slipped his finger over one intriguing responsive spot. His tongue corresponded with his fingers, entering and receding at the same time, at the same speed.

Squirming, she wanted more, needed more, but wasn't sure what it could be except for his rigid erection still pressed to her thigh. She wanted that, his more intimate part inside hers as she knew it should be. She rocked with him, into him, his mouth going wild over hers as their breaths mingled increasing to quick, sharp pants.

Suddenly, there was a tensing of her body. She felt internal muscles trying to hold his fingers in place, and the world shattered around her. Fireworks exploded behind her eyelids, her body tingled and tightened…but more than that. She knew she could never emulate the way her body arched to his, the way she felt this wave of ecstasy race through her and out the tips of her fingers and ends of her toes.

Holding her close with both his arms, he kissed her mouth gently, sweetly.

When she was able, she needed to speak. "Morris, that was indescribable. I had heard things, but no one came close to explaining. Now I know why."

He pulled her under his arm. "Time to sleep, Miranda. I'll make up my mind whether to stay or take you back to town. No one will be surprised either way after yesterday."

"What about you? You never…you never were satisfied, never climaxed."

"Sometimes it's not about the climax. I took great pleasure in bringing your body to life. I wanted you to know how it felt, and you are mistaken if you think I received no pleasure in what we did. I promise you I did. Now it's time to sleep—for both of us."

She snuggled against him, not wanting the closeness to disappear in the darkness. She knew morning would bring new things for them although neither of them could allow this to make a difference in their relationship. She wasn't wife material, and Morris certainly had no interest in being a husband. That would be the only relationship she would allow herself after seeing the women in Whitechapel and knowing how they got there.

CHAPTER TWELVE

Morris waved his carriage and driver off with Miranda safely tucked up inside. His decision had not been popular, but then he never told Miranda she would get a vote on how he ran this assignment. He had access to the house, the other guests accepted him, and she would be safer out of his influence.

Last night, he broke every promise he made to himself about how she would be treated under his protection. He had made a vow she would leave here as innocent as when she arrived. What she saw and heard was much as what she saw and heard in Whitechapel, but he had broken his own oath.

Not to touch her. Not to be tempted. Not to be the one to take her innocence. He came too close last night, and he didn't want regrets later. Or for her to regret meeting him. This way she had a chance of finding a man to marry, a man to love her as she deserved. Not a man called into service and sent to places like this country house party on a moment's notice. Where staying faithful to a wife would become difficult if not impossible.

He mounted his borrowed horse and rode in the opposite direction to rendezvous with his cousin, Westin. If anyone noticed them, it would seem a chance meeting between relatives. He would return to the party and select to make it an early night, accepting the ridicule of the other men for not completing his quest. At least his host would be happy with him since that man had won the wagers.

His horse loped over the even ground. How could he have treated Miranda so casually, so crassly? He was no better than the men who ogled her at the house party, the man who approached her in Whitechapel, that man Guthrie who prostituted her out through her writings knowing how much the income meant to her and her aunt.

His thoughts turned to their first meeting. How mistaking her for a man who had links to a group of anarchists led him to her door. He recalled the racy sexual scenes from her books, and his body parts took sensual notice of her. He thought about the library and her womanly scent, how he wanted to remain there in the warmth emanating from her core, and wanted to welcome her into the delights he knew he could provide.

But that wasn't what his life allowed or what she should allow. He would never be able to devote his time to a wife and family as she deserved. Something up until now, he thought he would never covet. But something about Miranda made him want to be a different man. A man who came home each night to his wife, perhaps children. Dine with them, play games with them, be a father like his was to him. No need to worry about the *ton* or their foibles. Not concerned with politics or the assignations of any of it. He wanted to be a second son of a second son.

Right now, that wasn't possible. He must meet his cousin and figure out who at the party was the danger to the royals and their way of life.

Westin was watching him with an unusual

expression on his face. "What has you so blue deviled? And who did you beat to a pulp? Those knuckles of yours look like it happened within the last day or so."

Morris' horse tossed its head at being held in place next to his cousin's larger stallion. "No one who matters to us. I may have misjudged my ability to tolerate bores and fools. It seems my capacity for both runs out after a day."

"Does this have anything to do with the young woman you coerced into helping you? I didn't approve of taking an inexperienced operative into a situation like that in the first place." He dismounted, giving Morris time to think of a suitable answer.

"She did better than I did, I fear. I allowed my personal feelings to get in the way, take precedence over the assignment, endangering the operation." He threw his leg over the saddle and jumped to the ground.

Westin was a little taller than he and wore a worried expression. "Did it have to do with the woman? Is the operation compromised?"

"No, she was instrumental in finding what we were sent to find—not the man involved although we found what he was looking for. A painting of the Tower had been placed in a locked room with a time and date on it two weeks from now."

"So, you think that date marks an attempt on the throne? Do you have an idea what it entails?"

"No, I think that information is held by very few, possibly by a single person. Again, the lady suggested I change the date to one sooner than that on the painting. Our insurgent will be at the Tower alone, expecting to take part in an activity to overthrow the crown. He, or she, will be easily taken by our agents, and we will get the information we are looking for soon after, I'm sure."

His cousin and superior officer still appeared worried. "Is everything else going well? You know you are my favorite of cousins."

Morris laughed at the often-told joke. "You don't like anyone. I have been thinking that possibly I'm not the best man for this job any longer. Not that I am resigning, but it has lost some of the glitter, I think." He mounted and turned his horse back toward the country house. "I will get these men and make them sorry they ever breathed air. The monarchy is safe, I feel it in my bones." He nudged his knees into the horse's sides, and it leaped into a canter.

****

The countryside slipped by quickly, too quickly. Miranda had to make plans, plans that did not include the handsome stranger she had shot. She made one decision. She would not be writing any more graphic stories for Guthrie. He could publish what she wanted to write or not, but she would no longer pander to men like those she found at the house party. The reprints would bring in funds for a while until she could find a publisher who would take on her more practical writings.

If she sold the clothes Morris purchased for her, she could afford to move her aunt to a village. They knew what kind of medicine eased the old woman's breathing now, and getting her aunt into the cleaner country air would be more help than any elixir. It would be a new start for them both.

Once in town, she had the trunk moved up the three flights of stairs and dismissed the driver and footman. Her aunt looked on with interest.

"Why I see you did a little shopping, Miranda dear.

You know I've been telling you for a while now you dress like a widow for no reason. It would be easier to catch a bachelor's eye if you dressed to emphasize your best assets."

Blushing as she told the lie, Miranda explained, "Lilly, my friend who was being married, thought these dresses were wrong for a married lady. Her husband plans to keep to his country estate so she ordered a whole trousseau made for herself."

Her aunt laughed. "And now she will probably become enceinte and won't be able to wear any of them. It always happens that way. Perhaps she will remember you are of the same size and send them on to you."

"Perhaps, but I have more than enough here already." To keep from continuing to lie to her best-loved relative, Miranda changed tactics. "Being in the country reminded me of how much cleaner the air is. I mean people were wearing white without the smudges that seem to occur here in London. I would like for you to consider moving to a village with me."

"I am not against the plan, dearest, but what about your job? Will you be able to transcribe for the courts if we live so far out?" Her aunt innocently reminded Miranda of all the lies she had lived these past few years to cover-up what she was doing.

"I have the opportunity to work in a different department, more along the line of writing. I can do it at home and make short trips to the city when I need to confer with a publisher."

Her aunt's face held a wide smile. "Then I believe we should move. I worry about you on these streets. The neighborhood seems to be going downhill at a rapid pace. I heard another tenant say someone was shot in this building. I mean what can we expect next?"

"Yes, what can we expect next?" Miranda said weakly.

****

"So, you are sure this Miss Donner isn't part of the conspiracy and has no direct access to those who are?"

Finding himself once more in the private offices in the home of the duke, Morris answered swiftly, "I have nothing to lead me to believe she is anything besides what she appears to be, your grace. I have spoken to her numerous times, and her sympathies do not seem to lean that way at all. The information she gave me and helped me to collect was from the source she accessed. I believe that woman, the woman I refer to as Number One, will be able to identify the men in question, and then I will pay her to live someplace safer."

The older man frowned, his bushy white eyebrows almost covering his stern gray eyes. "You insist on keeping Number One's whereabouts a secret even from me?"

"I do, your grace. That way the only way to her is through me, and I will not allow anyone access."

"And what if something happens to you? What then? No one will know where to find her, and the whole group may be lost to us." Duke seemed to speak his thoughts aloud, and Morris took no offence at the man's thinking so coolly of Morris' demise. It could have been the duke's own son, and the man would have thought about the operation to find the insurgents rather than one man's life.

"I bought the woman from her purveyor, and she readily went with me. The young woman in question has the address to come here if she does not receive any message from me in a specified amount of time. Just do not turn away any stray rag collectors or gypsies if I am no longer about. It may be this young woman seeking an audience with you."

The older man let out a rare chuckle. "You will have my poor butler leading every stray female who comes to my door here to my office? I should have you flogged for such an act."

"But you won't because you need this woman's statement in court. What she heard and saw will lend credibility to our charges. Without her, it is all hearsay, and nothing we have leads us to anyone killing Chesterfield."

"I just wish the man hadn't been so damn dramatic. Wanting to give me the information in private and in person. He could have given me the facts at the Winchell's ball instead of making a clandestine meeting for the next morning. The poor sod was dead by midnight and laying in the dark gardens of the Winchell's townhouse without any one of the hundreds of attendees any the wiser."

"It is no more than I wish, your grace. Everyday these men are free to plot and plan and possibly put those plans into action. We cannot prevent the royal family from going about their daily lives on merely a threat. Even, your grace. You have not curtailed your activities."

"The day I allow some upstarts to order my schedule is the day I am no longer fit to be a duke. I cannot be daunted by these men's plans although I have ordered my cousin to desist his seaside bathing with the public. I am glad the weather has turned cold so early this year. It has driven him back to town where we can watch over him better."

"And cold weather seems to be less induced to promote hot-headedness. The summer months more difficult to control mobs and such if that is the route they plan. Use the masses of unhappy commoners to create an atmosphere to push the monarchy or the House of Lords into doing something even more restrictive than the new laws."

Morris didn't need to watch what he said in front of this man. Whether he agreed or not, the duke would allow him the freedom to say what he thought. The duke knew Morris wouldn't act upon them or instigate others to do so.

"We cannot be sure this time. The French continued with their uprising for years through winter and summer. There was no season of war—it was all bloody chaos."

"I know you lost family members, your grace, and my sympathy is with all of those who gave up their lives. There are certainly safer and saner ways to lessen the burdens on the working class without bringing killing into it."

The older man became silent suddenly. Either thinking about his loss of friends and relatives or of the possible loss of more. Either way Morris felt his time with the duke was at an end for the day.

Morris stood and bowed. "I will keep you apprised of my findings whether positive or not. My usual manner will be used."

The man nodded his acknowledgment, but Morris knew the older man's mind was heavy with worry.

CHAPTER THIRTEEN

Miranda wrote from the scribblings on the notebook and leaned back satisfied she was finally making progress on the new book. She was thankful because her publisher wasn't an easy man to work for and demanded an exacting time schedule. He also demanded her total dedication to each project he paid for since he had paid an advance for the last two.

This one was already slated to be brought out before the holidays. Who he thought would purchase something this titillating as a Christmas gift, she didn't wish to know. She only knew she was on a tight deadline, and the time it had taken her to work with Mr. Mathews had put her behind once again.

That and the trouble she was having writing about the same subject. She was writing the salacious tale of a governess this time. It hadn't been difficult finding the basis for the story. A sort of Fannie Hill was the life of many of the women in the alleyways and corners. Young women trying to make a life for themselves in the big city while low life madams and pimps took advantage of their naïveté, as well as their poverty.

Miranda half-hoped her books would be used as warnings to these young women. To not trust those who may be trying to make money off the backs of these innocents. To stick to proper employment agencies and look before they leaped. Stay at parish houses and genteel boarding houses with strict rules. They were in place to protect the women until they understood the dictates of society as it was lived in the less elegant areas.

Pushing the finished sheets into a neat stack, she smiled knowing Guthrie would be content with the number of pages she was handing in and would release more funds. The medicine had become even more expensive. The vendor explaining the raw materials cost more due to taxes on the imported products. He blamed it on the Six Acts although Miranda couldn't figure out how laws concerning limiting the size of meetings and ownership of weapons could cause her aunt's medicine to become costlier.

Either way, she had no other choice besides pay it. Her aunt did seem better for taking it, and Harry couldn't find anything wrong with it other than it contained mostly alcohol. But then all such elixirs did. It cut the phlegm and allowed her aunt a few hours of uninterrupted rest. That was worth anything in Miranda's mind.

Miranda left her publisher's office and felt eyes on her. She hurried to the corner where she knew she would be able to hail a hackney to return to her apartment building. She should have paid extra to have the one she arrived in stay. Her publisher was so unreliable she didn't want to have to sit through one of his dissertations on how a real author should perform let alone pay for a waiting cab as well.

Now there was an urgency to be safely on her way home. Peeking from under her bonnet, there was no one who stood out as being threatening or of even paying attention to her. It was her own imagination running away with her. Writing about all those women taken from public places and forced into prostitution was giving her 'day-mares'. If she frightened herself every time she left the apartment, she would become a recluse.

Slowing her pace to a more moderate speed, she continued to the corner of the two intersecting streets. As she passed an alley walkway between two tall buildings, there was a blur from out of the darkness, and she was enveloped in a dust-filled canvas bag. Her arms flailed out hitting into a substantial body as she screamed only to have her mouth muffled by a large hand. A whack on the back of her head had her realize the reason men said they saw stars when punched.

She went slack, stopped moving hoping whoever hit her would think she was unconscious. It took all her might, but the grip the two men had on her told her they were prepared to do more against her if she fought them. If this were a kidnapping, her assailants would be after more valuable things than money.

Her clothing and finding her in the business section of town alone would let any abductor know she didn't have family rich enough to pay a ransom. These men were more nefarious than that. Miranda wrote about this type of kidnapping in her books. How some women became trapped in the life of servitude to their purveyors while living in shame and heartbreak when their own families turned their backs on them.

She knew what was to become of her, and she prayed she would take strength from the women she had interviewed, those who held out hope of escape, even some who had escaped. Like Lucy, who would not need to stay within the dirty district of Whitechapel any longer.

Once Miranda escaped, she would return to her aunt

who would welcome her back without blame, to Harry who would accept her explanation without criticism, and to Mr. Mathews who would say he told her so, but stand by her in friendship anyway.

Funny to think of him at this moment. To think she found him a friend when she knew he was interested in her in a much more intimate way. As she told him, she wasn't stupid—she was merely inexperienced. If these men carrying her through the alleys of the city had their way, that wouldn't be the case for much longer.

Trying to protect herself when she realized they were about to throw her into a carriage, she curled her head down as she landed on a covered floor. Even with the rough treatment, she couldn't let them know she was awake and possibly plotting an escape. How that escape was going to occur she had no idea.

Her feet were bound together, and her hands were inside the bag which was tied tightly around her waist. At least they didn't seem to want to molest her while the carriage was pitching them to and fro. Small mercies must be appreciated.

It gave her more time to think and make whatever plans she could. She must remain calm, not think about what was to come, only about what she could do to get loose, get herself free either now or in the future when a chance presented itself. She promised herself she would prevail no matter how long it took. Eventually she would leave the life these men were trying to force her into accepting.

Miranda could tell by the sound on the streets she was still in town, but now they were rougher with missing cobbles unreplaced. The odors were stronger as if the buildings and people were closer together, and what breezes made their way there never blew the foul smell of dirty men and refuse from the streets. Then there began a different stench she couldn't place, but which became stronger as they travelled the uneven lanes.

Rotting fish, that was it. There was a distinct smell of the harbor and the rancid leavings from the fisherman who gutted their catch and saved it to use as chum later in the day or in the lobster traps as bait. She tried not to gag as her mind and stomach fixated on the putrid smell and not on her precarious position.

Being on the docks was not a good thing. She could be taken to a ship and sent out with the crew as an incentive to remain with a captain as a form of reward. Sailors often abandoned their ship or captain once on solid ground, and one of those things keeping the men on land was that women were available to them. Captains used young women to lure these experienced sailors back on board. Whether the women lived through such an experience wasn't of importance, most often if they returned, they had the French gout so badly no amount of cure would counter the final end.

Swallowing her screams, she forced herself to think rationally. She didn't want to be hit hard enough to be knocked unconscious. If that happened, she may not wake-up until she was out to sea. She thought she could swim or rather float if she found a chance to throw herself overboard, but only if she were close enough to reach shore.

She had never been on an ocean-going vessel but had seen them and knew they were high off the water. She also knew hitting the water at the wrong angle could mean a broken bone or two, but compared to months at sea with a vessel full of rutting men was unacceptable. It would be signing her own death certificate. There must be a way to save herself because asking for help would fall on deaf ears.

If she found herself on board, would she be able to hurl herself over the side? She would do best to have her hands free as well as her feet. Could she pretend to accept her fate and lull them into believing she was so overwhelmed with fear she would be complacent? Could she keep her natural reactions to her capture and fear of her future from showing? She must put on a performance to save her own life. She must make them believe she was docile to her situation.

Too much thinking...too much thinking. She needed to focus on escaping and soon. Once she was onboard, there would be no escape, but she would have to be carried up the gangplank first. If she lay quietly until she felt the incline and then thrashed around, they may drop her, or someone on shore might investigate what they had.

With luck, she would bring attention to herself and pray someone would take the plunge into the harbor to save her. Although she remembered hearing sailors usually couldn't swim saying that if they were in the ocean, they were probably too far from shore to make a difference. Why spend all that energy when a shark was going to get them anyway?

She shivered involuntarily at her grisly thoughts. She must think of escape even if it took years. It was the advice she gave women like Lucy, and she must believe it will happen that way for herself, too.

The carriage slowed but did not stop. The men or man with her made no sound other than heavy breathing which made her think there was only one now. Other sounds interrupted her thoughts, sounds of machinery like the cranes used to lift cargo on and off ships and the creaking of ropes pulled taut as ships waited at anchor.

Perhaps she could escape one captor if she caught him off guard. Once the carriage stopped and he went to move her. Carry her up the gangplank. Possibly take her chances at getting them both into the cold water while she thrashed to free her hands. Would the weight of sodden slips and dress pull her down? Would the skirts wrap around her legs and prevent her from kicking herself to safety? The alternative could not be tolerated.

She could not live like those other women. She wasn't strong enough or brave enough. She never thought herself so weak as to welcome death before a chance of a life even if vile. She knew too much, and that knowledge had her planning impossible scenarios of escape rather than face life as a prostitute even if it were of her own making.

The carriage rocked to a sudden stop, and the sounds around her lessened. They were no longer on the main thoroughfare of the docks, but possibly an alley. Now would be her chance to figure out an escape by land. Before she was hauled onto one of the many ships set to leave port.

Hearing the man open the carriage door and call to another disheartened her even further. There was going to be more of them.

"Hey, Bart, get ov'r 'ere and give me a 'and. We weren't s'pose ta 'urt 'er none, and Pete 'it 'er so 'ard she's been barely breathin'. I'm not takin' the blame for this. 'is lordship ordered 'er brought to 'em alive and biddable. Whatever the 'ell that means. 'ow do ya steal a woman and make her biddable at the same time. And not be able to knock her 'round a little to soften 'er up, I mean."

Her feet were yanked by the ropes cutting into her ankles through the thin stockings. She hadn't realized until this moment that her ankles had swelled against the tight ropes, and her toes tingled with loss of blood. She placed her hands to protect her head as best she could and felt the two men pull her across the gritty floor. One grabbed her under her arms while the other carried her feet. At least they didn't let her head drop and hit the metal step.

They grunted with her dead weight and shuffled along the sandy pavers. The swinging of her body made her feel she was in a precarious position and flaying about now might have her dropped on her head. She didn't feel she owed this unknown lordship any thanks for telling them not to harm her since she would never have been in the position of harm if he hadn't ordered her brought to him.

Although not in a safe place, for some reason knowing it was a lone man giving the orders made her confident once again she would escape.

But who could this lordship be after all? She realized not all nobility had money to buy a woman, but there were several men involved in her abduction, and no one was trying to disguise that she was there against her will. There were at least four men so far that she knew of plus the man giving the orders, but why? Had she inadvertently caused a rich man's paramour to leave him? She always made the offer to help any of the women she interviewed. If not with money, she helped them escape to a home for women such as themselves or even a sympathetic priest who moved them out of the city and got them jobs in the country, back to where they started from, but much wiser.

If this man really was of the nobility, which she doubted, perhaps she could talk him out of whatever he had in mind for her. Talk him into dumping her back near the center of town where she would make her own way home. So far, she had no clue as to the identity of any of the men except for one very common name of Pete.

She was unceremoniously dumped and left once again on a hard surface covered with grit and sand. At least that was better than the bottom of the sea. She could take the time working lose the ties at her waist if she were able. Having her hands free and possibly able to loosen the knots at her feet could mean escape when the time presented itself. She noted she had thought when and not if. Remaining a prisoner was not an option.

She listened for any sounds. There were a few, but mostly the scratching of little claws as they ran around what must have been the perimeter of the room she was in. There was still the strong smell of the sea there. Not the smell of salt water spray, but more like the smell of the bilge-water pumped from the bowels of large vessels. Half human waste and half seawater from the many un-mended cracks in the hulls.

That was the other smell. Tar or sealer of some sort. She recognized it from when she was in Whitechapel. Near the cooper when he sealed his barrels to keep liquid from escaping the shrunken wooden slats. She must be in some sort of warehouse near the docks then. Probably along with the freight waiting to be dropped into the hold. She still may be destined for a sea voyage.

Miranda had done all she could do for now. She listened to the sounds of men moving around outside what must be the door, then the carriage drove off, and a steam whistle marking time. She could see no sign of light through the cloth sack so there were no windows, no way of escape besides straight out the door.

Miranda would wait for her chance and then make a run for it. She would not think what they would do to her if she didn't make it the first time. She would chart her own course and live or die by her own decisions.

CHAPTER FOURTEEN

Morris' valet met him at the door which was peculiar, but not completely unknown when they were working on a case of such importance.

"I couldn't find you, and the young lady you told me to keep an eye on has been taken."

"What do you mean taken?" he demanded, all thoughts of rest or food discarded.

"I had a street urchin watching the apartment building, like you told me to. I mean she's no longer a suspect, so I put her on a low priority."

"Yes, get to the point, man. Who took her and where?" Morris held his clenched fists to his side, but the man next to him glanced down and read the message.

Taylor expelled the words quickly. "The boy followed the carriage to the dock area, and she was unloaded into a warehouse."

"Why are you here then? You should be with her, helping her escape, man." He turned hoping to stop his carriage from leaving but found the street empty. "Come with me, and you can tell me everything you know. Where was she when they took her, how many men, everything. I must know everything."

Morris flagged down a hackney and threw a gold coin to the driver. Take me to the docks and be quick about it. There's another one of those in it for you if you make it in time for me not to miss my ship."

The driver tipped his hat and whipped up the horses before the door was closed. Morris' mind shifted to what he needed to know to save her. From what he wasn't sure, but he had to think it must do with the case he was working on. Somehow, someone else figured out she had knowledge that was pertinent.

By the time they reached the proper part of the port, Morris was familiar with everything the young boy had witnessed and passed on to Taylor. Although he couldn't keep up with the carriage carrying Miranda, the lad had caught up with the carriage when it became bogged down in the traffic that snarled the port area on a continual basis. Passengers, freight and sailors all vying for right of way to the harbor and its dozens of ships and barges.

Thank God, she hadn't been loaded on to one of those. Getting her safely off a ship was near impossible and one that may have set sail into the harbor, hopeless. He wasn't one to give up hope, and he knew Miranda wasn't either. She would fight to the bitter end. He needed to cling to the belief she would hold on till he came for her and not bring anything harmful upon herself.

Taylor pointed out one of the boys he had watching Miss Donner and knocked on the roof to let the driver know they needed to be put down. Morris kept his head lowered in case the men who took her recognized him and knew of his involvement with her and the reason behind it. He had added that worry to the others when he tried to reason why she would be taken off a very public and usually safe street. He kept returning to the same conclusion.

He was the cause of her being taken. He had led

someone to her door. Possibly someone saw them in Whitechapel together. Had seen her help him talk with Lucy and knew he had helped the street girl escape. He wouldn't put it past the pimp to have led these men right to Miranda. After all, that scum would take money from anyone, and if he smelled a deal, he would make it. No honor among thieves and all that tripe.

He and Taylor rushed to where the boy stood just inside an alleyway behind some empty barrels. The pungent fumes coming from them fought for dominance over the rest of the stench.

"Tell me which building she's in and if anyone is in there with her. I need to know my chances."

The lad tipped his cap while answering. "Gov'nor, I bin watchin' since I sent me mate to yer house and no one's gone in or out 'cept a nob. He din't look all that dangerous, or I might 'ave made a run for his purse just to get him to leave the lady alone."

Morris stared at the three-story building, judging his chances of ramming the side door which seemed to be the only entrance. Like many of the others along the wharf, there were only windows on the upper floor to discourage burglaries.

"What did the nob look like?" he barked at the boy.

"Not tall and not short, but dressed fancy and carried a gold-topped cane. If'n we kill 'em can I have the cane? It'll come in handy in a fight."

"You will be well paid for this, I assure you, but yes, you may have the cane because that gentleman will have no further use for it, I can promise you."

The boy touched the brim of his dirty cap again. "My thanks, gov'nor. What do you want me ta do? I can be a distraction, and I'm fast so those blokes guardin' the door will never catch me."

"That might help me temporarily. Let's see how much of a distraction we can cause."

****

Miranda tensed and ceased her activities as she felt the knots at her waist dislodge. She heard someone unlock the door. The pale shaft of daylight silhouetted a man's shape as he entered then disappeared. The rasp of a flint and a softer glow came from the same direction. A cultured voice emanated from the man now in the room with her.

"Well, now, Miss Donner. I find I am divided between learning what I need to know and the intriguing urge to understand how a young woman such as yourself could write such iniquitous stories. Are you self-taught perhaps and have been able to hide behind your aunt's slips all these years? How many times have you sold your virginity?"

She pretended to be unaware of him or his improper questions. She wasn't going to give him the satisfaction of defending herself or her morals. After all, she wasn't the one frequenting those places for personal pleasure. How dare he act as if she were some lightskirt or worse because she brought to light the poor treatment of such women?

"No, it is better you not tell me. I want to pretend along with you that our time together will be your first, and I still must find the reason behind having abducted you. How did you know about the house party and our little plans? We were very careful to circumvent anyone who wasn't in complete agreement with our cause. But then there it was in black and white—you wrote about the whole thing including the private meeting with just the few of us present. Meetings that were not meant to be known. Meetings once known outside our own circle caused some to back-out and declare they had no knowledge of such plans."

She remained quiet, trying to keep her breathing even. Hearing him move nearer, she worried that if he touched her, she would flinch and give herself away. She listened to his boots move against the gritty floor and then a chair scraping as it was pulled closer.

She breathed evenly although her heart was flapping like a bird in a trap, trying to get free, giving her momentum to fly at this man as well. Was he armed? Was there a pistol pointed at her as he spoke, never intending to let her leave no matter what secrets she told him?

He must have sat down. She could smell the burning oil in the lamp over the other scents, and she worried he would burn her alive if she remained quiet too much longer. All sorts of grisly death sentences went through her writer's mind. Sometimes it did not pay to have such a vivid imagination. The bard who her *nom de plume* was an anagram of was now the voice foremost in her mind— 'a coward dies a thousand times before his death but the valiant taste of death but once.' Not the best time to think of that refrain, but perhaps apropos.

Miranda stopped thinking about all the ways she may die and concentrated on the one way to live. Could she surprise him by throwing off her covering, perhaps even making it land on him giving her time to run through the door. She hadn't heard the lock being used when he entered, so perhaps it was still unlatched.

He kicked at her with his boot, evidently losing tolerance for her ignoring him.

"Listen to me, woman. I am running out of patience. I need to make a showing at the Winston's ball tonight and am not yet dressed. I need to know how you knew about the country house party and what went on there. How did you know to tell Mr. Mathews about it, and when were you going to ask for money? There would be no other reason besides extortion, or is Mathews paying you so well you won't need any other funds?"

He kicked at her once more and a pained grunt erupted from her. She was still trying to figure out if she were better off not answering him at all. The fact he had to leave for an evening event may mean he would leave and return later. Meanwhile, she could try to make a break for it. Before she finished with her thoughts, there was an almighty row outside the door. A young boy's piercing yell and scuffling, someone hitting the wooden door, and the jangle of the lock as it became involved in the melee.

There was a sudden cracking of wood, and something lightly brushed across her. The man gasped as he stood so quickly the chair tipped over and crashed onto the floor. Miranda tore off the stifling burlap bag and made a run out through the door which she could see was now a gaping hole of light amidst the interior darkness. The sun barely shown in the west.

No one stopped her wiggling out of the sack; no one stopped her from bending and pulling her legs out from the loosened ropes; no one paid her any attention at all. Scrambling to her feet, she barely glanced at the two men fighting, one with a sword and the other a large knife flashing in the light from the doorway. Racing through the aperture, she ran toward what she hoped was the exit of the alley, praying she wasn't heading to a dead-end and possible recapture or worse.

A young boy chased after her, urging her on which she didn't need to continue running as fast as she could, but appreciated his support. Holding her skirts up with both hands, she ignored the curiously surprised expressions from spectators and catcalls from men inviting her to run their way.

She ignored them, too. Concentrating on getting lost in the crowds she could see ahead of her. A busy street filled with wagons and carriages and coaches. She wouldn't stop running until she found someone familiar or a constable which she understood were thin on the ground in this part of London.

The boy tugged on her skirts and yelled out easily, "This way, miss. The guv'nors told me to take ya to his carriage that will be over here away from the fracas."

She took a good look at the lad and decided to trust him. He seemed to know who she was and that she had been held without her consent. She was sure he was the instigator of the melee outside the door of her prison causing her captor to be disconcerted enough for someone else to break through the large door and attack her tormentor.

Turning in the direction the boy was pulling her, hoping she wasn't going from the fry pan into the fire, she followed. The carriage seemed innocuous enough, and she allowed the boy to push her buttocks into the coach in front of them without letting down the slide-away step.

Sitting on the immaculate squabs, she felt guilty knowing she was less than pristine and the damage she could be doing with the state of her clothes. That is when she noticed the blood seeping into her stockings and made sure she didn't allow her damaged ankles to touch anything besides her own underskirts.

The boy slammed the door shut, and the vehicle ambled off without much notice taken of it leaving the crowded area. The place where it once sat waiting already occupied by a wagon needing to unload wooden crates. She pulled her head inside the window, finally sitting back and took a much-needed deep breath. It didn't relax her as much as she thought it would. She was now worrying if she had escaped one prison to be taken to another.

She considered how much it would hurt if she jumped from this height out of the moving coach. Nothing outside was familiar. There were two men on the driver's seat, and she held on to the strap near the door as she swayed and bounced with the speed of the vehicle now free to race dangerously down the wider cobbled streets.

CHAPTER FIFTEEN

The young street urchin ran into one of the men standing guard and clumsily picked the man's pocket before he continued to run farther down the alleyway. The man robbed, called out a crude comment and chased after the much swifter boy, who allowed the man a chance to catch-up to him while at the same time keeping just ahead of him. The altercation was seen by the second guard, but that man hadn't left his post to chase a boy who hadn't taken anything from him.

Morris came at the man full run, taking him down with the force of his punch and leaving him for Taylor to take care of. He had to save Miranda, and these other men were merely paid assailants and not cogs of the nefarious group trying to overthrow the government. He turned on his heel and rushed the door, splintering the hinges from the weather-dried casing. It crashed to the floor leaving the space open for his pursuit.

Seeing what appeared to be a heaving pile of rags on the floor, he realized it must be Miranda making her escape. He had to give her time to get away.

A man dressed as a gentleman stood so quickly the chair tipped backward making another crashing sound to echo through the cavernous room. His attention concentrated on the man who pulled a blade from the cane he carried.

The abductor in front of Morris was a little shorter,

and Morris accepted the challenge, pulling his knife from his boot. It wasn't a gentleman's weapon, but then Morris rarely considered himself a gentleman. This scoundrel was going to be surprised with what a trained man can do with a short blade. The length of a sword becomes a disadvantage in hand-to-hand combat. As soon as he was able, Morris dodged under the other man's arms and his sword's reach became moot.

Morris wanted to disarm the man, but not kill him. He needed this man alive to exhort information from him. Lists of names, places, anything to stop this group's plans from ever coming to fruition. Find out where their funding was coming from and who in the government was part of the insurgency.

While grasping the man's right hand that held the sword, Morris brought up his shorter blade and shoved it into the man's side missing the organs he knew would cause immediate death or cause the man to bleed out. He held himself back from the fury he felt for this man knowing he had been torturing Miranda in some way. Using the darkness and her fear of being at this man's mercy to frighten her. Probably to get Morris' name from her lips which she evidently had not given. It probably saved her life in not doing so. Once this man had the information he wanted, he would have killed her and have her body thrown into the harbor once night covered their activities.

Twisting the blade, he heard the hiss of breath escape the man he now held upright with his own strength. If he allowed the man to drop, the knife would do too much damage, and they would get no information at all. It wouldn't matter so much to Morris, but the duke would be furious to lose this one link to the others.

Pulling the knife out, Morris allowed the man to slide to the dirty floor with a grunt. He wiped the bloody blade off on the man's waistcoat which was quickly becoming saturated with the warm, gooey substance. He pushed the man's legs out of his way and called out to Taylor.

"Did she get away all right? Could you see if she made it to my coach?"

"Yes, she was in and away faster than a cat can lick its whiskers. The street lads are waiting just out of sight watching you take this bloke down."

"It wasn't a fair fight, but I don't need to play by gentlemen's rules when there are no gentlemen present." He glared down as the man moaned again, both hands pressed over the still bleeding wound, blood spurting out slowly with each heartbeat.

"Quit your moaning. If you brought a blade expect a knife fight. You're lucky I didn't have my pistol, or this would have been over much sooner, but no less bloody for you."

Taylor pointed to the guards. "I've got these two tied up with the help of the lads over there. Do we take them all to the magistrate?"

Morris shook his head and bent over to pick up the ropes Miranda left on the floor in her haste to take advantage of her captor being occupied. He found her reticule, heavy with coins. He smiled knowing she wouldn't think twice about running, knowing that discretion was the better part of valor.

"I have a special place for this one. Take those other two and maybe they will confess who else was being paid to kidnap the lady. The tower and rack are waiting for them. They will be hanged for treason once we know we have all the culprits."

The man on the floor moaned again and tried to speak. Morris pulled him to his feet and shoved him toward the doorway with the insurgent complaining more and more articulately.

"I'm going to have you hanged for attacking a peer of the realm. I have influence in high places. You'll be sorry you ever thought to interfere with my dealing with the woman. She's a prostitute and this was, but a little game we two play to make our love making more exciting." He sneered at Morris as if he thought his excuse was adequate to get Morris arrested.

Morris slammed his fist into the other man's face causing him to career into the door frame. Morris held him upright, snarling into his ear.

"Do not say another word to me about the lady. She is more noble than you will ever be. I know you are involved with sedition and the death of Lord Chesterfield. Since you have influence in high places, let's see if you can impress the Duke of Wellington since that is who will be leading the interrogation. He isn't thought a gentleman by many in the nobility. So, I raise you my duke plus a king."

The other man paled and seemed to have shrunk in size as well. All bravado was lost as Morris shoved the traitor toward the street and the prisoner transport waiting there with four constables, batons out and at the ready. They took the wounded man leaving the other two for another transport. Taylor and one of the constables left in a hackney with those two criminals while Morris went in yet another. He planned on being with the duke when the interrogation began.

****

Shivering, Miranda stood in the brightly lit foyer of a very grand home in St James. A butler looked at her rather oddly but didn't mention her disreputable state. Her hat was probably still in the bag once tied over her head. She could feel hair hanging lopsidedly down on one shoulder, and her gloves were long gone. Removed as she prepared to claw the man's face when she got the chance. She didn't even want to think of the condition of her dress and coat after being dragged across multiple dirty floors and alleys.

"His lordship sent word to expect you. The housekeeper, Mrs. Jessup, will show you to a room where you may clean up and rest." He turned toward a round older woman who hustled into the marble tiled room.

Sympathetically she cooed, "Oh, my dear. You must have had quite a fright. Come with me, and we'll get you all bathed and a nice pot of tea for you. Maybe a meal? I can have cook fix whatever you desire." She put her short arm around Miranda's back as she guided her up the curved staircase.

"Tea sounds wonderful, but I think the bath first. I do not know what I was hauled through, but I know most of the places smelled badly. I fear much of it clung to me and my clothing as well."

"Certainly. His lordship said to give you whatever you wanted."

Miranda wondered if this lordship was Mr. Mathews' superior? No, that man was a duke, and these people would be referring to him as his grace. So, this is another nobleman involved in saving the crown and protecting England's heritage. She would have to thank him for his concern on her behalf. After all, this wasn't of his doing. She was simply caught up in something she had no control over. And it seemed few others did either.

A tub was wheeled in right behind them, and buckets of steaming hot water poured into it within minutes. Evidently, they expected a grubby guest, or there was boiling water at the ready twenty-four hours a day. Probably the latter. Once the footmen left, the housekeeper helped undo the tapes at the back of the dress and made one pile of everything.

Wrapped in a towel, Miranda noticed her spencer was torn along a seam, and several ruffles of her underskirts hung loose. Mrs. Jessup rolled them all into a ball tutting about the damage to Miranda's ankles and the shredded stockings.

"I'll retrieve some ointment and gauze for those rope burns, miss. It's a shame a body isn't safe to go about their daily business without such goings on occurring. I don't know what things are coming to."

Miranda felt the urge to cry and wanted to be alone when she fell apart. "I'll be fine on my own. I bath myself all the time."

"Of course, dear, but I'll stay and help you rinse your hair out. I'm afraid there'll be a lot of snarls. Let me just pull out these pins that are hanging."

"Thank you, but I would feel better if I could merely get in the water and calm myself. It seems like it's been a rather long day."

"Yes, you do just that, dearie. I'll get the tea and be back to rinse your hair. Just lay back and relax as best you can." The woman hustled out. Evidently, she never walked anywhere even with her girth.

****

Morris hesitated to knock on the closed door

163

needing to make sure Miranda was unharmed. Mrs. Jessup explained there were bruises and scrapes along with some nasty rope burns which had been treated and wrapped. They would be uncomfortable, but not dangerous.

He still couldn't prevent himself from rapping lightly. If she were asleep and did not answer he promised himself, he would go away and leave her be.

She answered, "Come in."

He entered, and his gaze searched the empty bed before swinging to see her next to the window, the curtains pulled aside and the full moon's light shining in, haloing her head and acting as a beacon behind her. She sat curled up in the chair, a tea tray on the table next to her.

"Oh, Mr. Mathews, I wasn't expecting you. I thought it was Mrs. Jessup coming back to check on me. She has been so solicitous I feel guilty for keeping her from her bed so late. I know she must start her day early."

"She does, and I sent her to bed when I arrived home."

"Home? This is your home? But the staff refer to you as his lordship? What am I missing?"

"I find it easier when I'm working on certain things to use my mother's family name. My title is of little value to me. It was supposed to belong to my older brother, but he died during the last year of the war. I was called home but felt I owed the nation my loyal support and began working for the crown in various ways a simple cavalry officer never could have."

"So besides 'my lord' how am I to know you?"

"My apologies, Miss Donner. Let me make myself known to you. I am Morris Harrison, Earl of Heathton at your service." Bowing, he faced her once again unable to see her expression to this new information. He hoped she wouldn't let their difference in station rule out any chance of a friendship between them. He hoped for more, of course, and he had their liaison planned if she would be agreeable. They could even use the apartment she already occupied as a base for their rendezvouses.

"I would curtsy, but as you see, I'm not properly garbed."

He could not see what she was wearing, probably a voluminous nightgown borrowed from the much rounder Mrs. Jessup. "You are excused from the humbling of yourself. I never understood the need for such things myself, but, of course, I dare not speak such blasphemy. It smacks of insurgency and that hits too close to the crown these days."

He thought he saw a smile. "I understand. You must walk a tight line to remain in your position. What has your superior to say for today's, excuse me, yesterday's occurrences?"

"You think I ran right to him to relay the events?" He felt rather let down by her opinion of him as someone who needed approval from his supervisor.

"That is where you went, isn't it?"

"Yes, because we had to interrogate Lord Carstairs. He was a lynchpin in the insurrection. He knew all the others, and we now know who they are even if we do not know where they are. They hadn't gotten any further than accumulating like-thinking men, both of the nobility and others. Unionized men and even a well-known politician."

"Why me?"

"I'm afraid I may be to blame for that. When I

showed an interest in you, they did too."

She shook her head as if that couldn't be true. "But he, that Carstairs, mentioned me knowing about the original country house party and who went. He wanted to know how I knew the attendees. Even though I changed the names and made up their backgrounds, I must have hit some on the head. He was there and knew I wasn't, so he wanted to know who I spoke with to have so much information."

"So, he knows you are A. Haskepers? How do you think he learned that?"

"I think he got the information from Tobias Cutter, my publisher's assistant. He has never liked me and thinks my books are trash, which I will not deny. That is who you paid to get the information on the apartment, isn't it?"

"Yes. Evidently, I should have asked more questions. The man seems to be a font of information for the right price. I simply didn't ask the right questions. Such as is A. Haskepers, Esq. a woman."

Seeming to want to change the conversation, she asked, "This is your home then. What was the one I was taken to before, the one we left from to go to the country house party? Was it your mistress's residence?"

"No, but I often need to have a front of operations that is not directly tied to my title. People visiting at odd hours of the night would be questioned here in the family home. My staff there have no idea who I am really, only that I hold strange hours and am apt to bring unusual people home with me. Taylor floats between the two, just as I do."

They gazed at one another, neither saying anything more. Their need for the exchange of information satisfied while other needs remained unmet.

He broke the silence. "I should get to bed. I'll take you back home in the morning."

"There's no need although I would appreciate someone getting me a cab. I find I am a little nervous at the thought of being on the streets alone."

"I will be seeing you home, Miss Donner." He reached for the door before the urge to see her once more forced him to turn back. She stood when she thought he was leaving and was now silhouetted in the moonlight. Her torso and legs in vivid outline through the thin muslin.

Swallowing with difficulty, he tried to speak, "W-what are you wearing?"

She stopped in mid-step when he turned back. "Ah, Mrs. Jessup said her gown would be too large and brought me one of your shirts. It's a little large, also, but I can manage."

Long legs came from beneath the bottom of the shirt, and he noted the button holes remained empty. The studs unused since they would be uncomfortable to sleep on. The collar open where the cravat would have normally held it closed. Without intention, he took two strides and had her in his arms.

Lowering his head, he kissed her upraised face. She didn't pull away, nor was she shocked by his actions. Possibly she was expecting this. Possibly she planned on him finding her dressed as she was. She looked a wanton wearing only his short shirt.

Pulling her lower body closer to his, he felt her warmth, felt her curves beneath his hands which were roaming over her body freely.

Groaning with the relief of finally being able to

touch her, he kissed her. He brushed his lips against hers. She opened herself to him as another groan erupted from deep within him. He hadn't realized how much he had been holding himself back, refusing to allow himself to think of her as anything besides an asset. Someone to help him find the insurgents. Now he realized the fantasy of them being together was possibly more emotional than he thought.

"I want to take care of you. Dress you and give you jewels, a carriage and anything else you ever wanted. You would no longer need to write those blue-novels and demean yourself in front of men like Carstairs and Wyngate. You are mine, and I want to tuck you away in a townhouse where I could visit anytime I wanted."

Just the thought of having her to himself had him grinding his erection against her.

It took a couple of minutes before he realized she was no longer participating. She was standing there, but no longer returning his kisses. Her tongue wasn't bandying with his, and her hands were no longer on his shoulders. He gazed down into her somber hazel eyes.

"I'm afraid there has been a misunderstanding, my lord."

It took him a couple of more moments to climb out of the sensual haze he had worked himself into. To rid his body of lustful thoughts and pay attention to the reality that was slapping him in the face.

She continued, standing in his embrace, but leaning away from his aroused body, "I am not one of the characters in my books. I created those women from little snippets of many others needing salvation. I did not mean to have you assume I was interested in any manner of their way of life."

Stepping back, he dropped his hands. "I, ah, I apologize for my forwardness. It must have been the reaction to finally having the men I searched for under guard. I was grateful for your help. I'm also relieved you were not more seriously hurt before I reached you. Please, get some sleep, and as I said earlier, I will escort you home in the morning."

This time he did leave and pulled the door closed with him. He leaned against it, his back rigidly straight kicking himself for being so foolish as to opportune a young woman who had only been involved in this fiasco due to her inadvertently writing about a country house party. An advent that had begun the entire demolition of an insurgency that could have brought about the end of England as it was now known.

He couldn't rest even after all that had occurred that day. The fears and fights and worry of finding Miranda unharmed had built him up, and now he was deflated. Unable to understand what he would do. What he should do about this woman he had such strong feelings for…more than mere feelings. Words got in the way of his thoughts although he knew what he wanted. He wanted to keep her in his life, and yet, how did he go about doing so?

The young lady certainly hadn't seemed to wish to be part of his life. She seemed to have an adversity to the nobility and all they stood for. How did he bring her into the life he led? A king's man dedicated to saving the monarchy while putting his own wants and wishes on hold.

Of course, there were duties he had that could preclude the other at this point in his life. Having a wife and family would make it less complicated to move about in society. No one would suspect a married man of espionage. Even the king would agree.

So, he was speculating about having a wife…no, not any wife. He wanted Miranda. Had always wanted Miranda, but couldn't admit it even to himself. Admit there was something he wanted as strongly, or more so, than to be of service to his king.

Miranda had never berated his work or expected him to leave it. She had never done anything to make him feel as if what he was doing was beneath him. She hadn't even bulked all that much at being used to help his mission. Wasn't a woman like that one in a million? Wasn't a woman like that worth fighting for?

He would become half a man without her in his life. Less of that half if he could no longer meet with her…speak with her…touch her if even for a moment. He could see a future without her, and it was bleak. One he did not wish to face. One he did not want.

The only thing to do would be to change her mind. Convince her that living as his wife, anywhere she wanted, wouldn't be a bad thing. His love could breach any differences in their station or class. He found no reason to keep them apart… The problem was in convincing her.

CHAPTER SIXTEEN

Morris met Miranda in the foyer. She was without a hat or gloves, but he handed her reticule to her. "I'm sorry. I forgot about finding this yesterday."

"It is the final installment of my book earnings unless it goes into a second printing like the others. That is what I was doing downtown that day. Was it only yesterday afternoon? Somehow it seems so much longer ago than that." She put her hands through the braided handle and smiled as if nothing untoward had happened to her.

"Shall we be off then?" He ushered her toward the front door.

"Yes, my lord, but could the butler pass on my gratitude to Mrs. Jessup? She cleaned my entire outfit and mended the tears. I deeply appreciate all she has done for me and on such short notice."

His butler relaxed enough to smile and bowed slightly. "I will make sure she knows how pleased you were with her service."

She stepped out the door and walked toward the enclosed coach of the night before. This time she used the lowered step and sat facing backward, leaving the front facing seat for him.

"Come sit beside me. I don't bite," he teased feeling the constraint between them and hating it. He preferred when she thought of him as plain Mr. Mathews. Now he was 'my lord,' and he wasn't happy with the situation. He wasn't sure why, but he knew he wasn't happy to be taking her home without any reason to see or speak with her again.

When his carriage stopped, Miranda stepped down and turned, blocking his exit from the coach. "No need to dismount, my lord. Please thank your staff for me and for anyone else involved in my rescue. I truly appreciate the danger they placed themselves in for a stranger to them."

"Miss Donner, I said I would see you home, and I intend to do so. Please step back to give me room." He was angry she didn't wish to be seen with him, as if now that she knew he was of the peerage he was abhorrent to her.

She went up the few steps to the front door, quickly inserted the key, and left the door open behind her. As she climbed the narrow stairs, her dress swept the steps clean. She tried to brush him off once more when they reached the apartment she shared with her aunt. She gazed into his face and her lips pressed together in restraint, he was sure.

"Miss Donner, I will see you safely home. And I think I should speak to your aunt. After all, you spent the night in my home."

Her eyes became round as she gasped. "You wouldn't say such a thing to her, would you? I mean, she is an old woman and would not take hearing such things lightly. That was the whole reason for the second apartment so she would never see what I wrote. Never know that I wrote. She would not understand the need and I do not want her to think her illness is forcing me to do unlady-like things."

A frail voice called out from behind the door. "Miranda? Miranda is that you. Did you misplace your key?"

Opening the door, Miranda gave him a warning look. "No, Aunt Agatha, I merely ran into a friend who felt the need to walk me to the door."

"You must have gone out early. I didn't even wake when you left." The old woman said as she shuffled toward them. She wore a voluminous nightgown with a well-worn robe over it and a lace-trimmed bed jacket over both. Making her way to a comfortable looking chair, she sat down heavily.

Evidently Miranda wasn't going to allow him past the door, so he took it upon himself to do his duty. "It is Morris Mathews, also known as Morris Harrison, the Earl of Heathton."

Pushing past the surprised Miranda, he made his bow toward the older woman.

Miranda rolled her eyes and completed the formal introduction, "Lord Heathton, the Dowager Baroness, Agatha Woodard."

It took a moment for the words to sink in. Miranda's aunt was a baroness? Why was he just learning of this now? Why hadn't any of this come up before?

He turned briskly toward Miranda and accused, "You kept this from me. Who are you really? I want the real name and the name of your parents."

If Lady Agatha thought this conversation was odd, she didn't say so.

"I am waiting, Miranda," he said, holding his back stiffly, his temper barely under control.

"My name is Miss Miranda Donner. I have left being the daughter of Viscount Trowbridge behind me.

We are not part of that life any longer. Cannot afford to be part of that life."

"You belong to the peerage," he stated defeatedly. She moved about the room, picking up and then setting down items such as books and a hairbrush.

He caught up with her and forced her to stand still. Speaking quietly, he said evenly, "You know this changes everything between us."

"There is nothing between us, my lord. You needed help with a problem, and I gave you aid. There is nothing more to be said. No one owes anyone anything. May I see you out? I need to get my aunt's breakfast around. She does best in the morning, and I like to take advantage of that to have her eat a substantial meal at this time."

He bowed and turned to the door, but *sotto voce* said, "I will return later this afternoon, and I expect to be received."

"We shall see if I am at home, my lord. The past two days have been very draining for me."

He left her with a stern expression. He would brook none of her dodging him any longer. She had kept this piece of information from him deliberately while he treated her with less than courtesy. He took the sets of stairs at a brisk pace. There was much for him to think about.

Her father was a viscount—her aunt the wife of a baron. Her credentials, entry into society was as good as his yet he had dishonored her. He promised he wouldn't take advantage of their need to be close, and at the first opportunity, he had done just that. He didn't like himself much at this moment.

****

Miranda was hurrying back from the apothecary. It

had taken longer this morning to get her aunt settled after breakfast. She had questions about Lord Heathton, of course, and Miranda was having difficulty being ingenuine with the woman who had cared for her all her life. She owed the woman the truth, but what was the truth? That they were as poor as church mice and to earn money she decided to use the only talent she had—the ability to write?

And that ability hadn't been appreciated by publishers as she had presented it. Only being able to turn information garnered from women who had chosen another path for the similar problem gained Miranda enough money to live on. And then only if she were very frugal.

Thoughts of their small two-room apartment, her cot behind a screen in one corner and a small sink and counter in another. She hadn't seen it as it really was until Lord Heathton left this morning. Then she saw it as he had. Small, squalid, and in need of paint as well as a carpet. The only thing it had going for it was that it had water from a tap and a drainpipe to rid itself of the same.

Being on the top floor meant too many stairs for her aunt to climb. The poor woman was a virtual prisoner in her own home. Harry was the only one who visited besides the doctors she could coax to check on her aunt monthly for a few extra coins.

She rounded the corner, hoping her aunt was still napping. It had taken forever for them to mix up the elixir this time. Her stomach dropped as she saw the now familiar carriage in front of her apartment and the driver and footman waiting next to it.

Without glancing their way, she hurried up the steps and into the small entry. She wore her second-best hat and her aunt's gloves until she could replace the ones she lost. Looking up the stairs, she began climbing as if facing the gallows. On the second set of stairs, she realized Lord Heathton was alone with her aunt and that spurred her feet to move faster so that she arrived at the door breathlessly.

It was unlocked, something she never did, so she pushed into the room. Her aunt was sitting in the cushioned chair, and there was a smile on her face. Miranda couldn't remember the last time she had seen her aunt smile like that. Certainly, not during the past year. There was a grimace of pain more often than not.

Miranda approached the two people talking cozily to each other.

"Miranda, dear, come sit by me. Morris was just telling me about his grandmother, and do you know, we came out the same year. I remember her and how she loved to dance. She said she chose her husband because he was the only one who could keep up with her at a ball."

"I'm glad you have been having such a nice talk. You aren't getting tired, are you? Do you need anything? A cup of tea?"

"No, I'm fine, dear, but perhaps Morris would care for some. Do ask."

Shaking his head, he answered the unasked question, "No, I came from lunch at Whites, and they always do such a large meal I often skip supper as well."

She felt unable to meet his gaze which she felt rest on her. She couldn't figure out why he had returned. He had been assured she had recovered from her ordeal and only needed to return to her ordinary life in her ordinary way.

He stood when she entered and now remained upright. "Miss Donner, Miranda, I would wish a word with you before I leave, if I may?"

She knew it wasn't a mere request. He meant if she wanted him ever to leave, she better make time to speak with him. Giving him a tight smile, she turned to walk him to the door.

"I came to ask your aunt for your hand in marriage, but then thought better of it." She was just recovering from the shock of his admission when he finished, "You are the one who has the power to grant me my fondest wish—that you become my wife."

This time her voice abandoned her. She could feel her mouth open and close, but no sound left her. She tried again, "Mr., I mean, my Lord Heathton, have you lost your senses?"

He seemed confused. "I must have done something wrong. Let me try again. Miss Donner, will you do me the honor of be…"

"I got that, you fool. What I mean is what is wrong with you that you would make such an offer to me. I am not a proper lady to be a countess. I live in a hovel. I work for a living at a job that would be offensive to all, but the most liberal of thinkers, and I am too old."

"How old are you?" he asked seriously.

"Old enough that I should be wearing a white cap." As he kept staring at her she answered mulishly, "I am three and twenty. I am past the pale and well on the shelf."

"I can deal with that. Plenty of years to get children on you." He stated and she couldn't tell if he was being serious or trying to goad her into taking him to task.

Gritting her teeth, she tried not to bare them as he

focused on her eyes.

"Now what were those other reasons? Oh yes, you wrote for a living. Well, you would not have to make your living so you would write whatever you chose under a *nom de plume* or your own which would be mine. So, we are set on that one? And as far as living in a hovel you, of course, would be living in my hovel. I expect your aunt to move in as well. There will be plenty of space here in London and in my country home, even with all the children."

Now she knew he was teasing her, but not in a mean way. He seemed to be serious.

"I appreciate the offer, I truly do, but such a move would cause so much controversy and if my secret ever got out, you and I both would be ostracized. My life has been as a tightrope walker. One misstep and it would all come falling down."

He shrugged. "I run around as if I were a spy, which is not acceptable work for a peer. I was in the military, and now work whenever the crown feels it needs a man to go into the bowels of the country and dig out insurgents and nefarious beings. I walk a tightrope as you so rightly put it, but always with one foot in polite society. I do not need to tell you that plenty of the righteous peerage would not do well if all their dirty linen was exposed. Ours is nothing compared to those others."

"As I said before, I must decline your offer. I fear we will not suit."

"I have not accepted my congé, so this is fair warning—I will return." A moment passed without a comment from her, so he finished, "Is there anything I can do for your aunt?"

"No, I have more of her medicine. That and fresh air is all the doctors recommend. But the air is too full of soot here in town, and I cannot afford to take her anywhere cleaner. I was hoping to, but it will depend on how well this book sells. I do not have a contract for another, although my publisher sounds promising."

He bowed slightly picking up his hat. "Feel free to contact me at home anytime. Jessup will know my whereabouts." He bent and placed a quick kiss on her surprised lips. He was out the door before she could protest, and she quickly turned to see if her aunt had seen them. By the smile on her face, once more, she had.

Early the next morning, too early for visitors one would think, Miranda was disturbed by rapping on her door. Harry would not be needing her since he would be in class, and there honestly wasn't anyone else who it could be. She almost told whoever it was to go away through the door.

He must have heard her footsteps approaching. "Miranda, let me in. It is urgent I speak with you directly."

She glanced over at her aunt who had fallen back to sleep already. Often that was the result of taking the elixir. Unlocking the door, she whispered so as not to wake her aunt, "Go away and come back later. I am not receiving company."

He pushed the door open wider, stepping though while looking behind him as he closed the door. "My valet reported that I am in the papers, well, that we both are. There is speculation as to who I was with in an enclosed carriage the other day down at the harbor. Someone must have seen part of what occurred and twisted it to meet what they think happened. Someone added that I had been down there to pick up a disembarking Russian Princess who I will soon marry. Others say I was with a beautiful courtesan who looked, er, well-loved when she finally descended from the coach in front of my home."

"Oh. Oh, dear. I'm sorry to have put you in this position." She worried her lip with her teeth trying to come to terms she may have been recognized and her secret profession may be exposed as well.

He spoke quickly. "I can weather the close observation. It is you who should be worried about being found out. I cannot tell them what I was really doing there. The government has decided that all insurgencies be kept hushed-up. They do not want to instill unsettlement and conjecture among the people. To learn there are peers also in conflict with how the country is run would be detrimental to the whole balance which is precarious at best. The regent isn't popular with his over-spending, and the old king is brain-sick most days. I came directly here to warn you, and I saw a reporter I know across the street watching this place."

"He saw you enter? The carriage?"

"I'm afraid so."

"How did he put you and I together? How would he know to watch me of all people?"

"Perhaps through Carstairs, possibly someone recognized you or watched me bring you home the next day. I don't know, but these men make their living ferreting out much larger secrets than we have. After all, we weren't exactly being clandestine about the whole thing. We both are now known in Whitechapel. Someone is bound to put it together, and then all hell will break loose. You and your aunt would have to move if nothing else. And someone might make problems with your publisher for printing the writings of a single female of the peerage."

Her hand went to hold her head which ached past the point of endurance. "How did I ever get into such a mess? I simply needed to write to earn some money to support us."

She was angry and guilty for possibly causing her aunt upset. And she most certainly would be upset when she learned what Miranda had been doing this whole time.

"Let me announce our engagement. Better yet, we should be married as soon as possible and then they will focus on that. Once we are married, we are boring news no matter how we met."

Staring at him closely, she realized somewhere along the line he had taken hold of her hands which felt cold in his warm ones. She tried to think of some other way. Some other way to keep her aunt from learning about her writings and some other way to keep from forcing Morris into a marriage he would soon regret.

"Can we simply announce our betrothal, and then I will allow you to bow out in a few weeks?" she asked weakly knowing the answer before he opened his mouth.

"An earl does not jilt his intended nor does he allow his intended to jilt him. Be sensible and look at reason. The only way to keep the cover on the plot, your aunt ignorant of what you've been doing these last few years, is to marry me."

"What if I am recognized by someone who saw me in Whitechapel? More than once, I ran into men I didn't know, but who certainly appeared to be nobility."

"Then you explain your dedication to seeing women

like Lucy find a new way of life. You can use your notes to write pamphlets edifying these women's plight instead of for the salacious reading of those who should be helping them and your greedy publisher. We can use the money you earn to start a charity or donate it to one already struggling for help."

He kept hold of her hands, and she felt him lightly squeeze them waiting for her answer.

She closed her eyes saying a silent prayer and when she opened them, she nodded in agreement. He leaned down and kissed her eagerly before stepping back.

"I will put it in the papers and get a common license. We will be married the day after next if I can find the bishop and he is available. It doesn't matter. Any clergy will do as long as it is done quickly."

A croaky voice called out from the chair near the window where the weak sunshine could find her. "Miranda dear? Are you kissing that nice young man again? Does this mean you will finally get married and give me great, great nieces and nephews? Is that the right connection? Well, you know what I mean and what I want."

"We both do now, Aunt Agatha," she answered although she didn't move because her hands were still in his.

Everything moved quickly yet smoothly. It was whispered to the press that Morris had known Miranda for years. That his grandmother and Miranda's great aunt, Lady Woodard, had known one another and come out together. A hint the two older ladies had always hoped the young people would make a match.

Miranda laughed out loud at the audaciousness of the newspaper article, stating everything as fact without knowing anything for truth. Each reporter wanted to be the first with some new tidbit concerning the couple of the hour. She thanked Harry for bringing the paper to her. She explained at that time she was marrying mister, well, Lord Heathton.

"I shall keep my mouth shut about how you actually met. I would get into such trouble if I was found practicing on a live human patient before I was licensed. Working on a cadaver could put me in prison for life, working on a peer of the realm must be a longer sentence." Harry teased when he was told of her upcoming marriage.

She looked at her only friend. "I never doubted you, Harry, but if there is anything I can ever do for you, do not hesitate to ask. My intended owes you for saving his life that night."

"I thought you told me you would have taken him to a hospital if I hadn't been there to help."

"I think I would have. Although at the time, I thought he was a burglar with questionable motives. I only recently found out he was an earl."

"That probably makes you about even since he didn't have your name right either to begin with." He smiled cheekily grabbing a biscuit as he left.

CHAPTER SEVENTEEN

Morris paced his room nervously as any prospective husband might on his wedding day. He had purposely stayed out of sight of his bride-to-be so she couldn't back out of their agreement, well it was more his agreement than hers. He knew it needed to be his idea, and Miranda might need a little time before she agreed his plan was the best one for all concerned.

Checking the clock on the mantel again, he found the hand had only moved ten minutes.

This wait was excruciating. Not the waiting so much as the fear she would renege, that he hadn't given her strong enough reasons for marrying him. That he had feared rejection so had not told her his emotions were involved. He loved her and hoped in time she would love him in return, especially after the children began to arrive. Doesn't a woman always have strong feelings for her children's father? He was betting on that fact although he could think of several close friends in which the rule did not apply. Look at the regent. He doted on his daughter while his wife wasn't allowed to attend the same functions as him.

But what else could Morris do? Miranda's occupation was bound to come out if the news journalists kept searching for the mystery woman. People could remember them together at some point, or the publisher would scent a story and write a scandalous piece himself

184

to generate interest in her books.

The clock was now five minutes closer to the hour.

Perhaps he should go down and join the bishop and the few close friends including the duke who showed way too much interest in his bride to have Morris comfortable. He expected Miranda would stay in her room until she was sent for.

He descended the stairs with his stomach still in knots of worry. He hoped he appeared calm outwardly. It would not do for his prospective wife to think he was in any way other than pleased with her becoming his wife. She was skittish to say the least. Of course, he could always hold her aunt hostage until Miranda married him.

He had sent two good sized footmen and a Bath chair to fetch Lady Woodard for the ceremony. She was to be placed in the chair, and the men were to carry both her and the chair down the flights of stairs to the coach. They had then wheeled her to the spot she was in now near the front of the room, rows of chairs already filling-up behind her. He caught her gaze, and she smiled giving his confidence a boost, hoping the lady's goodwill mirrored her great niece's.

The string instruments stopped for a moment and then began the processional march, the one indicating the bride was entering, and everyone stood and turned to watch. As they waited a polite hush went over the guests. And still no bride.

Instead, his valet who had been coordinating the event came down, trying to appear less than his six-foot-four as he sidled toward Morris whose heart sank. Had Miranda balked—or worse—ran? He forced a smile to the group and leaned into his valet to listen. He nodded and smiled once again to the guests indicating they should take their seats once more.

He strode past the now curious guests and into the foyer where he was told his bride waited to speak with him in private. Taylor was right. Not a footman, nor Jessup nor a housemaid in sight.

Her beauty took his breath away. Her hair was swept up higher than she normally wore it. There were narrow braids looped from the sides to the top and appeared to be holding the rest in place. Little cream-colored pearls were placed strategically around the curls as adornment. The dress itself was like butter cream with lovely lace covering it all. He couldn't have chosen one better if he had a year to do so.

Reaching out, he took her gloved hands in his and felt her tremble. Nerves then. That was all it was. She had become frightened facing a group of strangers, members of the ton.

"You are lovely, and everyone is anxious to make your acquaintance. They are all eager to get to know you, and you will like them in return. There is not a mean spirited one out there, except the duke, but he usually saves his bad manners for me."

"Morris, listen please. I am not afraid of them. I am afraid of you. And somewhat of myself. I have lied to you," she confessed as tears wet her cheeks.

"Darling, I don't care." He wondered if possibly she wasn't as innocent as she once claimed. They hadn't talked of it again because it didn't matter to him. "The clock starts over right now. What matters is what happens from now on between us. I don't need to know. I don't wish to know anything else."

"But I feel I must tell you. I do not want to start our

married life with a lie between us. One that may grow and ruin any friendship we try to build." And he was lost as a tear rolled off her chin. He caught it in a handkerchief he had the sense to pull from his pocket.

Placing his arm around her shoulder, he lowered his head, preparing himself to hear the worse, to forgive the worse, and then marry her. "All right I am prepared to listen. Tell me everything so we can move forward."

"I love you," she told him in a wavering voice.

"What did you say?" He thought he misheard.

"I love you, and I didn't want to enter into this marriage without you knowing. I am not trying to obligate you to feel the same, but I thought honesty was the only way to begin a marriage. I didn't mean to love you, and I know it is not the done thing among the *ton*, but I am not made that way. I wouldn't be here if I didn't love you. If you feel that is too much to bear, too much responsibility on you, I will understand if you wish to call off and go our separate ways."

The tightening of his heart caused pain in his chest. "My darling, foolish girl. You have made me the happiest of men." At her astonished expression, he laughed and pulled her closer. "Not because you would let me cry off, but because you were honest enough to let me know you love me although not as much as I love you. I was going to let me grow on you hoping you could care for me, allow me to father your children and then in the future hopefully find we rub along together quite well."

He kissed her gently, not wanting to mess her dress or hair. Aware there was a room full of people who might come out to see what was holding up the main entertainment.

She seemed leery of his motives. "You're not simply saying that are you, Morris? I know you are kind in that way."

"No, I love you. Have loved you and no matter who you were or are now, I would insist on marriage. I have had more than a few agonizing nights thinking about you wearing my shirt. I would like to have the knowledge of you out of that shirt and in my arms."

Blushing, she nodded. "I am ready then. Tell them to begin the music again."

****

Morris clicked the door closed and faced the bed, his wife sitting on one side with her back to the headboard. His thoughts ran over the racy, sexual scenes of her books, and his body parts took more sensual notice of her. Her elaborate hairstyle was now brushed smooth, and her jewels put away for the night. He could see something white and frothy beneath the sheet that she had pulled up to her neck.

He kept his banyan on, covering what he planned on wearing to sleep, which was nothing. He didn't wish to frighten her with a full-blown erection, not after her experience with women who had been abused by men. She might not take it as a sign of desire, but one of violence. He hadn't thought this part out very well. He loved her, wanted to make love with her, but they had never discussed their preference for intimacy.

She spoke first. "Are you as nervous as I am? I mean after all those interviews you would think I would know all about this. You know, man and woman being together."

"Since we promised to be honest with one another, I'm nervous, too." He wanted to assure her. "I know what to do, but I don't want to frighten you, remind you of what other women went through with men who didn't care about them."

"But that's the difference. I mean you love me, and I love you so I am not afraid of you in that way. I know the basics, well much more than the basics and much more than the usual young woman of the *ton* would know."

He chuckled as he climbed in beside her and sat with his back against the headboard, as well. "Does that mean I might not meet the criteria? I'm not very adventurous when it comes to these things."

"Then we can learn to be adventurous together. I like the idea of that. Learn from one another and choose what bits and pieces we enjoy."

"I don't know if you mean it to be, but your inspirational talk has me thinking all sorts of thoughts. Many of which I would be willing to try tonight." He leaned over to her, placing his arm around her back and pressing his mouth to hers.

She reached her arms around his neck. "I could do this all night long. I was afraid kissing you only felt good that one time, but I think I like it anytime."

"Then we can kiss anytime. To hell with what anyone else thinks, we make our own rules. Rule one is you may kiss me anytime you feel the need."

"I like that rule. M-m-m-m, rule two is we may touch one another anytime." She petted the soft mat of hair on his chest then stroked her hand lower over his stomach muscles under the banyan.

He let out a hiss. "Rule three is neither of us wears clothing to bed." He slipped the banyan off his shoulders leaning forward to free it before tossing it on the floor next to the bed.

She did not hesitate wiggling to lift weight off the lower portion of her gown, pulling it over her head, then dropping it next to her side of the bed. Lovely as it was, he didn't miss seeing the gossamer cloth hiding the pink areola of her breasts slip away. Now both were peaked and pointing up, inviting his mouth to take a taste.

Lowering his head, she cradled it. He suckled one breast. His other hand waking and initiating the other to his caress. She arched and offered more for his pleasure. He slid her body down onto the mattress half covering her body. Going from one taught nipple to the other, he stroked his hand lower over her flat stomach and to the mound that was the center of her being.

His touch made her pause in her stroking him, petting him and learning his body as well as he was learning hers.

"I don't want to hurt you, so when you want to stop, tell me. This is further than I thought we would ever get this soon. I love the feel of your hands on me. I love the feel of you under my hands, and I love you. What I never want to do is push you into doing something you don't want or aren't ready to do."

He continued to kiss her breast and then returned to kissing her mouth, dueling with her tongue and imitating the sexual act by thrusting and retreating.

Sliding his middle finger into the wet warmth between her legs, the satiny feel almost undid him as he arched his hips against her thigh. He wanted to enter her and pump deeply, but knew he must hold back. Her first introduction to lovemaking had to be right, not some demonstration that he could not control his passion.

When he returned to kissing her breasts, and being

satisfied rubbing his finger deeper into her channel, he groaned in frustration and need.

"I'm ready. I can tell I'm ready," she urged him, trying to slide under him.

"I can wait if you need me to."

"I want to join with you. The best part is joining with someone you love. And I do love you. I know it will hurt some, but then it gets so much better. I trust you not to hurt me more than you need."

Her hands pulled down on his bare buttocks, and he moaned as he took her mouth in his again, positioning himself before penetrating the entrance made for his body.

She pulled away and he stopped moving. Then she pushed upward and finished breaking the hymen. He waited for some sign she wanted him to continue, and she gave it to him. He worshiped her with his body, joining as man and woman were meant to join.

Within moments he felt her internal muscle clasp his erection, and he emitted his seed knowing they were reaching the pinnacle together. That neither would be left behind or disappointed. He shuddered to a release as she collapsed under him, dropping her arms to her side in euphoric abandonment.

He waited a moment then slid to her side and pulled her against him allowing their breathing to return to normal.

"Is it always this good? Is this what all the women said they would choose over everything else. To be with a man they loved?"

"I think it is always this good between people who love one another. I am sure I have never felt so close or complete."

"I know you have to rest before we can do this again, but I think I'm going to like being a married woman." She kissed his breast and nuzzled into his chest hair.

"Rule number four, we don't need to wait to continue making love. Didn't I read a part about a certain man who liked to do certain things to a woman so he could keep from getting her with child. I think I recall something about special kisses lower—lower—lower. He slid down her body, and her hips lifted off the mattress when he found his mark.

EPILOGUE

"Miranda, darling, where did I leave my spy glass? I want to see what those children are up to in the orchard. I warned them not to climb the trees even though it sounds like fun. Falling out of one isn't."

"Oh, Morris, that's like trying to tell a grasshopper not to jump. There are no trees in town in their neighborhoods, so the children find them fascinating up close. To climb a tree must be second nature to a boy."

"I understand that. It's why we have these weekends for the older boys at Haskepers House. They get a taste of country life and learn about farming and horses. Their mothers get a respite from their older children whinging they are bored in town or getting into trouble."

"Perhaps I'll make enough on this next book to pay for a couple of horses at a nearby livery in town. These stories aren't as profitable as the first four were although I enjoy writing about romantic couples finding happiness ever after."

She protected her eyes with one hand while trying to see as far as the orchard. "Perhaps the older boys can work there to help pay for the mounts. You know riding time for each hour put in working. We can figure out how it works later."

Picking up the spyglass, he aimed it toward the orchard. "There they are. They are not climbing now, but I swear they were when I first thought to check on them."

"Come back to the picnic, darling. They all must return early today since school will begin for them tomorrow. Let them get some good country air into their lungs. It's done such a splendid job with Aunt Agatha I am quite sure she will be here when this baby is born." She consciously splayed her hand over her rounded stomach.

He peered down and dropped next to his wife on the carpet brought out for the picnic. "I'm glad she will be here with us longer than the doctors had first indicated. She has gained a little weight, can walk farther on her own, and isn't coughing as much. All is well in my kingdom."

Smiling, Miranda added, "Rule number twenty-seven. We will enjoy our time with just the two of us because once this little one comes, there will be much less time alone for us."

He kissed her stomach. "Rule number twenty-eight. I will never regret getting you with child so soon after our marriage. I look forward to being a father as well as a husband. A truly committed married man."

A word about the author...

A voracious reader her whole life, author Susan Payne loves the written word. When reading more than fifty books per month wasn't enough, she decided to allow her mind to take flight and write all the many stories that kept intruding in her life. She blended her love of history and her love of words to create over eighty stories. All historical and centering on a couple finding love and a happy ever after together. www.authorsusanpayne.com

Thank you for purchasing
this publication of The Wild Rose Press, Inc.

For questions or more information
contact us at
info@thewildrosepress.com.

The Wild Rose Press, Inc.
www.thewildrosepress.com

www.ingramcontent.com/pod-product-compliance
Lightning Source LLC
Chambersburg PA
CBHW070506260626
47161CB00004B/1474